Tam Morgan, *The Liveliest Girl in Salem*

Tam Morgan

The Liveliest Girl in Salem

by RUTH LANGLAND HOLBERG

Illustrated by PETER SPIER

DOUBLEDAY & COMPANY, INC., GARDEN CITY, N.Y.

For
Christian,
Tycho,
Jannik,
Trina
and Steffen Von Rosenvinge

Printed in the United States of America

Copyright, 1953, by Ruth Langland Holberg
Library of Congress Catalog Card Number 53-5046

jH 688 t

I take this opportunity to thank Miss Florence M. Osborne
of the Essex Institute Library for her invaluable help
in locating material for this book.

My thanks also to the Peabody Museum.

Tam Morgan strutted the length of one of Salem's smaller wharves whistling "Up with the Bonnets of Bonnie Dundee." It was her father's favorite tune and hers too. She was so full of energy that her short red curls bounced as if they were on springs. The sun made them glitter redder than ever.

Tam reached the end of the wharf and peered down at a small fishing boat. It was rocking gently on the tide that sloshed and slobbered in and out between the piles that supported the wharf. Her whistle never let up. A man cleaning his morning's catch raised his head and chuckled. "Knew it was you long before I sighted you. That's a fine tune you whistle. I mind me of the time when your pa and I were boys in Scotland and we heard the bagpipes skirling 'Up wi' the Bonnets o' Bonnie Dundee.' The men were mustering, and we followed them until they chased us back home. It's a brave fighting tune."

The fisherman shook his head. "They don't have tunes like that now'days." He selected a fine haddock and held it up to Tam. "Here's your dinner, lass," he said.

Tam sprawled on her stomach and reached down to clutch the fish. It was wet and heavy and it slipped from her hands.

She tried again to grasp it more firmly. "Mac." She leaned over so far she nearly lost her balance. "Mac," she grunted, "hand it up so I can get my fingers in the gills. It's your fault I dropped it."

"Hold your temper, lass," Mac warned, "or you'll come over headfirst and land on my catch."

Tam scowled. At that moment she heard a boy's voice shout, "Redhead! Gingerbread!"

Tam scrambled to her feet as soon as she had the wet haddock in one hand. She glared at the boy. It was Jeff Carter. She felt her temper rising higher and higher. It was a grand feeling. Her light brown eyes flashed, and before she knew what was happening she threw the wet haddock at Jeff, and it hit him square in the stomach.

Cherry

Jeff had the wind knocked out of him, and it was some minutes before he could talk. Tam stood with her bare feet planted far apart, braced for the attack she was sure would come from Jeff.

Mac stood up in his boat. His head was about level with the floor of the wharf. He saw Jeff kick the haddock over the edge of the wharf. "There goes your dinner, Redhead," Jeff shouted. Then he turned and walked carelessly down the wharf until he came to one of the rickety buildings where a watchman sat on a barrel, half asleep in the warm September sun. He stopped a moment to tickle the sleepy watchman with a straw and then he went on.

Tam was disappointed. Jeff didn't think enough of her to have a tussle. Tam clenched her fist and felt of the muscle in her upper arm. "I've got to

get stronger so Jeff will fight with me. I wish, oh, how I wish I wasn't a girl. I hate cooking and sweeping and wearing skirts."

Tam was mumbling and looking so miserable that the fisherman called up, "Don't take it so hard, lass. I'll give you another haddock." He thought Tam was disconsolate because the haddock for her father's dinner was now the dinner for a crowd of screeching, hungry sea gulls.

Tam burst out, "He wouldn't fight with me. I'm getting bigger and stronger all the time and I could give him a good fight, as good a fight as he gets with those boys he runs around with."

Mac shook his head in disapproval. He thought to himself what a pity it was that Tam's mother had died. She needed a mother to train her to act like a girl. Thomas Morgan didn't know how to bring up his motherless daughter. He had two small boys to worry about besides, and nowadays Thomas was giving all his thoughts and devotion to the brig he was building for Captain Jacob Cromwell.

"Here you are then," he called to Tam. " 'Tis a fine haddock but not as big as the other. Bake your father an oaten bannock and give him a hearty dinner. He looks pookit."

Tam hated cooking, but she loved her father,

and to have Mac say that he was pookit meant that he was starved-looking. "I'll cook him a big hearty dinner," Tam promised. She flopped down on the wharf and put her fingers in the gills of the haddock. "Thank you, Mac," she said, and gave him one of her best smiles.

"Lass, when you smile like that," said Mac, "I almost think you're pretty."

"Humph," Tam snorted. "I don't want to look pretty. I want to look just like——" She stopped talking. She wasn't going to tell Mac that she wanted to look just like Jeff Carter. She stood up and thrust out her chest and held her chin high. She strode along the wharf, too busy with her imitation of Jeff to realize that as usual she would be late with her father's dinner.

Thomas Morgan was already home poking up the fire and looking into the pots that hung on trammels over the smoldering ashes. They were empty except for one that had some stiff cold corn-meal mush left over from breakfast. He added a dipper of water and commenced to stir it over the hottest part of the fire that was beginning to blaze up. He was hungry. It had been a long time since breakfast. Shipbuilders in Salem rose early and worked from the first light until dark. He wished his daughter would come home. He wanted to send her to the woods to pick up a basket of tree-nails.

Tam was as useful as a boy in many ways. She should have been a boy. There had always been a firstborn son named Thomas Morgan as far back as he could remember. He had been disappointed when his first child turned out to be a daughter. His pretty little wife was sad, too, and she insisted that the daughter be named Tamesine, the Scotch way of pronouncing Thomasine. Two boys had been born later, Nathaniel and small Jamie. Then two years ago a terrible sickness had swept over Salem. It was a tropical fever the crews of several vessels had brought home with them. Thomas Morgan's wife was among the many who died during the epidemic.

Thomas Morgan sighed. He forgot to stir the mush. He thought about the two small boys he had taken across the bay to Marblehead. An old aunt of his wife's was boarding the little boys and bringing them up as best she could. But the noisy boys made her nervous. She complained to Thomas, "I'm stiff in my joints. I'm too old to trot all over Marblehead for those rascals."

"Keep them a bit longer," Thomas begged. "I'll take them home when they are older. I can't manage now with the brig I'm building. It must be finished as soon as possible. Captain Cromwell depends on me to keep the men at work from dawn to dark."

Old Aunt Tabby put her nose in the air. "You don't need to point out my duty to me, Thomas Morgan. The poor motherless boys would have no care at all if left to that harum-scarum Tamesine."

At that moment the door flew open and Tam came in whistling. "Up with the Bonnets of Bonnie Dundee." She slammed the fish on the table. Then she saw her father crouched at the fire. A faraway look was in his eyes. She sniffed.

"Mush is burned," she announced.

Thomas Morgan woke from thinking about his problems.

"Aye, aye," he stammered. " 'Tis burned."

Tam saw his troubled expression. At once she forgot her plans to be as strong and tough as Jeff Carter.

"Father, I'll get your dinner cooked right away. I didn't know it was so late."

She flew around with a brisk air, and Thomas Morgan eyed her with a wry smile. Tam had promised that very morning when he went off to the shipyard that she would have his dinner ready for him and have the hearth cleaned and the beds made. But as so often happened, Tam forgot her promises because she found something more interesting to claim her attention.

Soon there was a sound of frying and the odor of fresh fish taking on a crisp brown crust. Tam took care to prepare the food well. She couldn't help noticing her father's troubled mood. During dinner she spoke cheerfully. "Father, what would you like to have me do for you this afternoon?"

Thomas Morgan pushed away from the table. He had eaten a hearty dinner and now he began to feel better. "Take a basket and go to the woods and get me some trunnels."

Tam grinned. That was going to be fun. "Locust wood makes the best trunnels, doesn't it?" she asked.

Her father nodded. "Yes, and oak makes the best wedges."

Tam propped her chin on her hands, elbows on table. She spoke seriously. "Jeff Carter says treenails instead of trunnels. He is wrong, I told him."

Thomas Morgan looked surprised. "Well, in a way he is right. But all shipbuilders call them trunnels. Children learn these things from schoolmasters who are too fussy about how to talk properly."

He gazed at Tam. "I suppose you should be going to school this winter. You didn't start school at the proper age because you had to stay home to

17

take care of the boys while your mother was sick. But I need you to keep house. When this ship is built I will have time to look around and find a housekeeper or someone who could come in to cook and clean—not that I like the idea of some strange woman in my house."

"Father!" Tam cried out. "I don't want to go to school. You have said yourself that girls don't need to go to school. You said all a girl needs to know is how to cook and sew and keep house and bring up children."

Thomas Morgan laughed. "But you don't like cooking and sewing and keeping a clean house." He pointed to the dusty hearth and to the floor that should have been sanded in a fancy pattern if Tam had been making proper use of her time.

Tam frowned. Maybe her father would send her to school if she did not spend more time keeping the house neat. That wasn't what she wanted. She wanted freedom from all responsibilities. Freedom to roam the wharves, to putter around the harbor in a dory or hunt the woods for white oaks that would be made into ships' planks. She wanted to help her father the way a son would help him.

"Father"—she was quick to think up a way to turn his mind from schooling for her—"read me that piece you put in the Salem *News*," she coaxed.

18

Thomas Morgan, the Master Builder, picked up the paper and read parts of the advertisement. " 'Let every man in possession of a white oak tree be ambitious to be foremost in hurrying down the timber to Salem. Your largest and longest trees are wanted, and the arms of them for knees and rising timber. Four trees are wanted for the keel which together will measure 146 feet in length and hew 16 inches square. Please to call on the subscriber, who wants to make contracts for large or small quantities as may best suit and will pay the ready cash.' "

Tam's eyes glowed with admiration. She was proud of her father's reputation for being a fine shipbuilder. "I'll go now and find some locust wood for trunnels and I'll look for white oaks, too, that are tall and straight with arms branching out to make proper ships' knees."

Her father nodded and hurried off with a businesslike manner. He had forgotten everything but the ship he was building for Captain Cromwell. Trees were coming into Salem from Danvers, Peabody, Beverly, and other small towns. They were hauled on drays or on sleds in snowy weather, drawn by slow-moving oxen. Thomas Morgan walked rapidly down Browne's Lane and turned into Whitefoot's Lane and down to the shipbuilding cove near Cromwell's Wharf. He had to see how the men in the sawing pit were ripping the long logs into planks.

Tam never gave a glance at the greasy dishes on the table. She took a basket and dashed down the lane. It was a long trip to the woods. She ran or skipped most of the way, her short red curls bobbing up and down with every motion. She didn't stop to look in the shopwindows but tore along like a whirlwind.

The Reverend William Bentley, out for an afternoon call on some parishioners, admired her brilliant curls and radiant health, but he sighed to himself, "That girl needs a mother and other girls for companions. She is always running around with boys and she is growing too old for that. I must invite her to accompany the next group of children I take for an instructive nature walk. Perhaps a walk along the shore and a talk on shells and stones and fish, or perhaps flowers and mosses, might better awaken her to the interests suitable for a female."

Tam, all unaware of the good man's plans to reform her, had reached the woods and was busy breaking off branches of locust wood into suitable lengths for treenails. Her basket filled, she looked for white oaks but found none because it began to grow shadowy and it was time to return home.

Tam walked steadily. The basket was heavy, and she could not run with it. When she reached the tobacco store with its wooden carved Indian in front, she put down the basket and stopped to pat the tobacco leaves the Indian held out. The Indian had been carved by Moses Carter years ago.

She suddenly became aware of someone leaning in a corner. She looked sharply. It was Jeff Carter, the son of the wood carver.

"Jeff! What are you doing here?" she greeted him boisterously.

Jeff did not reply. Tam came close to him. "What is wrong?" she asked. "Are you angry? Are you mad because I hit you with a wet haddock this morning?"

Jeff was sulky. He grumbled, "Pooh, that was nothing." Then because Tam's amber eyes were bright with her admiration for him, he broke down and told her why he was angry.

"I earned enough money to buy a hat, a real man's hat, and I wore it home. My father took one look at it and threw it on the floor and kicked it to pieces."

Tam gasped with sympathy. Jeff went on, "He gave me money to buy another hat, but he says my mother must go with me the next time I buy one."

21

"What was wrong with the hat?" Tam burst out.

Jeff scuffed his feet on the ground. He didn't want to tell what was wrong with the first purchase he had made, but Tam persisted. "What was wrong with the hat, Jeff?"

Jeff poured out his tale of woe: "The hatband had been stuffed and padded to make it fit my head. It was a big man's hat. My father said only a rascal would sell a boy a man's hat and cheat him like that, and he says I should have had more sense."

"Oh, Jeff, I think you have sense. I think you have more sense than any boy in Salem," Tam declared. "I think you are wonderful, and I wish I was as smart as you are and as strong and brave."

Jeff grinned. He began to feel better. "You are smart and strong. I guess I know how strong you are when it comes to throwing a haddock."

"Feel my muscle." Tam offered her bent arm and clenched fist to Jeff.

"Pretty good for a girl," Jeff said after feeling the bunched-up muscle.

Tam flashed a gay smile at him. She picked up her basket and hooked it over her arm. "Trunnels for my father," she said.

"Treenails, you mean," Jeff said. "That's what the schoolmaster calls them."

"Trunnels, trunnels, trunnels!" Tam sassed back, and went at a lively pace down the twilight-shrouded street toward the cove, screeching, "Trunnels!" until she was out of sight.

When Tam reached the shipyard, the carpenters were beginning to quit work. They greeted her with rough cheerful voices and hurried along to stop at the tavern before going home. Tam sniffed the air. It smelled of bark and oak chips and tar. She stopped at the sawing pit to see what was going on. It was a deep pit, and a staging was set up across it and a log was lying across the staging. One man stood on the staging astraddle the log, and he was facing opposite to the direction of the saw cut. He held a long two-man handsaw. Below him in the pit was another man facing the direction of the saw cut to avoid getting sawdust in his eye. By alternately pulling on the saw they ripped up a log into planks.

Tam loved the smell of fresh oak sawdust. She watched the men saw the log into the last plank. It was getting almost too dark to see, and they worked furiously to get the plank finished. This timber would be seasoned in salt water. No unseasoned wood ever went into any boat built by Thomas Morgan.

Tam's father came to stand beside her. His face crinkled into a smile of approval. These men were the most skillful sawyers in Salem. There was a third man, who shifted the log now and then so that the saw would clear the staging.

The plank was finished now, and Tam watched the men get ready to start for home. The man in the pit climbed up a rope ladder. They stopped long enough to take a look at Tam's basket of locust wood for treenails. Enos Higgins chucked her under the chin. "You have bright eyes for the proper wood. These will be pegs that will last. Did you mark any white oaks?"

Tam said, "It was growing late and I had a long way to come home, so I didn't look for any."

Enos laughed. "It was time to cook your father's evening meal, you mean."

Tam was dismayed. She had forgotten all about the evening meal and she suddenly remembered the unwashed dishes and all the other chores she

26

had neglected. The men went off whistling in anticipation of a bracing drink at the tavern and after that a good hot meal at home. Tam looked sideways at her father, wondering if he was going to say something about her forgetfulness.

Thomas Morgan was looking beyond the shimmering water flooding up in full tide. His eyes were fixed on Marblehead. There the dark green pines stood stiff and regular against the darkening sky. The sound of small lappings at the water's edge was mournful. The masts of a ketch lifted against the sky, and small fishing boats swayed at their anchors.

Tam slid her grubby hand into her father's large hand. She loved the solid rough feel of it. His fingernails were worn down from handling lumber and tools. No amount of scrubbing could ever get them free of the tar and oakum that blackened their rims. There was a warmth and comfort in his hands that spread through her body. She leaned her head against him and pressed her tangled mop of curls against his coat. For a few minutes they stood close together.

Thomas Morgan said, "Eh, lass. Someday we will have the wee boys at home with us and not over there in Marblehead. Come now, 'tis dark."

Tam tucked the basket of treenails under a plank

27

where they would be safe. She crunched over the dried seaweed, and once she stepped on a dead fish that had been washed up. Her father led the way.

The church bells were ringing to mark the end of the working day. Thomas Morgan turned into Derby Street, which was crowded with men. Tam could tell that one sailor was just off a ship because he walked with a rolling gait as if he were still on his pitching ship. She spied a dark-skinned man with earrings who was dressed in brighter colors than the other sailors. Her eyes were always eager to spy out sailors from other parts of the world. Suddenly she pulled at her father's sleeve.

"Listen!" she cried. "I hear music. Somebody is playing a fiddle."

"Aye, but come along," her father said.

"And dancing! I hear their feet," Tam persisted.

"You must not stop and listen. The Reverend William Bentley preaches against such pleasures," Thomas Morgan scolded.

Tam moved along, but she did not turn her head to see where she was going. She bumped into a gang of men coming from a tavern. The open door brought a strong smell of rum and stale beer. Thomas Morgan waited while Tam got herself untangled from the gang of men. He stared into the tavern. He wanted to go in and enjoy the noisy

29

companionship of men home from long voyages to China or the Indies with exciting tales to tell of the ways of other people.

Tam's eyes were big with curiosity. "Let's go in, Father. I see two sailors dancing a hornpipe. I can dance a hornpipe too." She gazed at the sailors in checked shirts and dungarees. They wore glazed black hats with trailing ribbons. It seemed to her that all the fun in the world was centered in that noisy room.

Thomas Morgan was suddenly stern. He took Tam's hand and rushed her along the street until they turned into Browne's Lane. The small house stood dark and forlorn. Not until the candles and whale-oil lamps were lit and the fire stirred up did it seem like home. Tam yawned widely. Then her eyes fell on the unwashed dishes. She glanced at her father. He was bringing in logs for the fire and a bucket of water. She felt cross and tired and hungry. She fried ham and baked johnnycake. There were some cold baked beans to warm up and a bowl of grapes and some sweet yellow apples to top off the meal.

Finally, when Tam could hardly keep her eyes open, she called her father to the table. He was moody and spoke little.

Tam's head was so full of sleep that it fell forward. She jerked awake. There were dishes to be washed before she could go to bed, and she remembered that the beds had not been made.

When Tam finally finished her work she was too cranky and sleepy to say good night. More than ever she resented being a girl with a girl's work to do.

She slept heavily. At five o'clock her father shook her awake. "Time to get up, lass," he said over and over before she opened her eyes.

"Father," she murmured, "I was dreaming. I dreamed that the brig was to be launched and——" She sat up straight. Her eyes sparkled. "I was christening the ship, and a great crowd of people cheered when she slid off the ways. I named the ship——" She stared into space. "Father! I can't remember what the name of the ship was." She burst into tears and blubbered, "Oh, why did you wake me?"

Thomas Morgan patted her on the shoulder. "Tam, it was only a dream, and you know dreams are not real. Dreams never come true. Besides, a little girl never christens a ship. Now be a good child and get up. The fire is hot and I'm hungry for breakfast."

Tam brushed away her tears with an impatient gesture. She seldom cried. She hated crying girls.

"But—but it seemed so real." Her voice was sad and puzzled.

In a few minutes her clothes were on and she pattered on her bare feet between the fire and the table. Her father eyed her suspiciously. "Did you wash your hands and face? I can see that your hair has not been combed."

Tam sputtered, "I'm clean enough. I scrub hard Saturday nights, and that keeps me clean all week."

Thomas Morgan bent his head over a steaming bowl of bean porridge. Tam was so determined to have her own way that he was almost ready to give up trying to change her into a more obedient and respectful daughter. He did not relish the frequent squabbles they had over her rude boyish manners.

When he left the house to go to the shipyard, he did not tell her as usual to sweep the floor, nor did he give her any orders for the day. Besides, she seldom kept her promises to clean the house.

Tam was surprised that he had no orders for her. Her conscience pricked her, and it was an uncomfortable feeling. She immediately set about putting the small house in apple-pie order. Somehow she didn't mind it as much as usual because her dream was still vivid in her mind. She kept trying to remember what she had named the ship just before it slid off the ways into the water. Tam even washed the outward-opening windows with their small diamond-shaped panes set in lead, and that surprised the neighbors. When Tam spread the washing over the currant bushes and on the grass to bleach in the bright sun, the neighbors nodded with satisfaction. Maybe that wild girl of Thomas Morgan's was mending her ways and staying home to tend to her duties.

But after she gave her father a hearty dinner at noon, the neighbors saw her prance out of the house, whistling and tossing her red curls as if she hadn't a care in the world. Now and then she would give a high screech because it was so wonderful to be outdoors again.

Tam galloped down to Cromwell's Wharf. It was one of her greatest pleasures to prowl around the huge warehouses with their queer spicy smells floating out to tantalize her imagination. There was always a watchman eager to tell about the goods stored inside.

Peg-leg Jeggles greeted her. "Got a piece of rock candy for you, Tam."

Tam grinned. Peg-leg was a crony of hers. He had a wooden stump strapped on one thigh and he was as nimble as a lamb in springtime. Tam thrust the chunk of rock candy in one cheek, and its

33

sweetness began to run down her throat. She mumbled, "What smells so strong, Peg-leg?"

"Ho," he chuckled, "that is cinnamon, cloves, and nutmegs. Captain Cromwell, he's in there getting out some of those little woven baskets of foreign spices to take for a birthday present to his mother. His last ship brought in rolls of satin from China and rolls of blue and white seersucker and nankeen from India and sprigged blue and pink muslin for little girls' party dresses."

Tam frowned. "Pooh—party dresses. Not for me. What else is in there?"

Peg-leg rolled the words on his tongue as if he were tasting them. "Dates from Africa, ummm. Figs and raisins from Spain. Wine from Madeira." He smacked his lips and wiped them with the back of his hand, as if he had just been drinking wine. Tam giggled.

"What else?" she urged him on. But before Peg-leg could go on describing the goods from faraway countries, the door of the warehouse opened and Captain Cromwell stepped out, followed by his old colored man and his cook laden down with presents for the captain's family and relatives.

Tam bobbed her head respectfully and stood aside for him to pass, as all Salem children were taught to do for a sea captain. She raised her head then and stared at the handsome young man. He had gray-blue eyes under strong brows, a high-bridged nose that denoted a quick temper but a generous mouth, and firm lips that showed he was a just and fair man in dealing with his crew. Captain Cromwell wore a tall white beaver hat and a high white stock around his neck. He wore all the fashionable garments of a prosperous man ashore.

Tam's cheek still bulged with the slowly dissolving chunk of rock candy. Captain Cromwell gave a curious look at her lopsided face and then at her ragged skirt and bare feet. Peg-leg saw the captain's eyes twinkle. "This is Thomas Morgan's lass," he explained.

"Oh," Captain Cromwell joked. "A chip off the old block, eh? Red hair and all."

Tam grinned with delight. Then she choked on the sweet syrup running down her throat. She got red as a beet and almost burst with coughing. Peg-leg pounded her on the back, and she spit out the chunk of candy.

Captain Cromwell took a box of dates from his servant and broke open the top. "Here, eat a date. That will help you to swallow properly."

Tam took the date and chewed it down as best she could. Then she managed to croak, "Thank you, Captain Cromwell." She bent down to pick up her bit of rock candy.

Captain Cromwell was stunned. "You mustn't put that dirty piece of candy in your mouth. Throw it away."

No one ever disobeyed Captain Cromwell when he used his shipboard voice. Dismay showed in Tam's eyes as she threw the delicious candy into the water.

Captain Cromwell held out the box of dates. "Take this home with you, girl. What is your name?"

"Tamesine." Tam's voice was meek.

"How old are you?" the captain questioned further, sizing her up from head to toe.

"Nine years, going on ten," she said. Then she added, "Sir."

"Humm, I have a daughter, Felicity, about your age, but you are bigger in every way than she is." The captain smiled. Then he turned smartly on his heel and went off at a dignified pace, followed by his laden-down servants.

Tam and Peg-leg Jeggles turned to each other with one idea. That was to stuff down as many dates as they could. Peg-leg saved all his date stones while Tam tried to see how far out she could spit hers.

"Why do you save your pits?" Tam mumbled with a mouthful of sweet sticky paste.

"I'm going to carve them into tiny monkeys," said Peg-leg. "And say, here comes someone."

Tam turned around. It was Jeff Carter.

"Jeff!" she screeched. "Come quick and see what I got—a whole box of dates from Africa. Captain Cromwell gave them to me."

Jeff eyed the dates suspiciously. He had never

eaten one, but he had seen them displayed in a store on Main Street.

"What do they taste like?" he asked.

Tam's sticky mouth spread in a wide grin. "Sweet and kind of mushy when you chew them," she said.

Doubtfully Jeff ate one. Tam and Peg-leg watched his expression change to one of satisfaction. Jeff and Tam spit out their stones to see who could spit the farthest. Peg-leg's pile of stones amused Jeff.

"How can you carve monkeys out of those little pits?" he asked.

Peg-leg explained that he had learned to carve when he was on a whaling ship. "We carved all sorts of tiny trinkets from whalebone," he said. "When I was laid up after losing my leg that a whale bit off, I had plenty of time on my hands."

Jeff's father was the best carver in Salem, but he carved figureheads for ships and cabin moldings and fancy scrolls for the ships' trimming.

Jeff bragged, "My father is starting to carve the figurehead for Captain Cromwell's new ship over there." He pointed to the shipyard, where the skeleton of the new ship lifted against the bright afternoon sky.

"I want to see what he is carving," Tam demanded. "Let's go now."

At that moment a cry went up that was heard every workday at eleven o'clock in the morning and again at four o'clock in the afternoon.

"Grog-ho!"

The men working in the shipyard or anyplace on the water front were served a mixture of rum and water. It was considered a healthy drink and it put spunk into the men just when the working day seemed endlessly long. Their employers allowed no loitering after the drink.

Peg-leg went hopping nimbly to get his cup of grog, and Tam put the cover on her box of dates. It was more than half empty now. They called good-by to Peg-leg Jeggles and trotted down the wharf to Derby Street and then up Hardy's Lane to the Carters' house. Jeff pushed open the gate. It was a pretty yard, which Tam admired. It had tall lilac bushes and rosebushes that still bore a few last roses. There were flower gardens all kept very neat inside brick borders. The house was weathered with age, steep-pitched, and the second story overhung the first story. Back of the house was a ramshackle building where Moses Carter was chipping away at a block of elm wood.

"Pa," Jeff called. "Here's Tam Morgan come to see the new figurehead for the ship her father is building."

Moses Carter was a small nervous man who darted about the huge chunk of wood, peering at it through half-closed eyes. Now and then he would stand away from it with an anxious expression, and then he would spring forward to chip off a tiny bit here and there. For quite a while it seemed as if he hadn't heard Jeff. Then he turned quickly to the children.

"Can't you see I'm too busy to be interrupted?" he began in a peevish voice. Then he glared at Tam for a moment and his eyes grew sharp.

"Come here. Stand there." He pointed to a spot on the floor.

Tam was puzzled, but she obeyed.

"Don't move. Turn your head more this way." He took her head and pushed it around as if it were

a wooden doll's head. He poked up her chin. "Keep it like that," he ordered.

Then he made a sketch of Tam's head with charcoal on a large sheet of paper. Tam stood as if glued to the floor. Above the scratching of the charcoal and the muttering of Moses Carter she could hear the sound of men chanting in the distance. It was the chanting of the ropewalkers from Shallop Cove Road. They sang as they walked with a wad of combed fibers wrapped around their waists. A few fibers were attached to a hook on a spinning wheel that another man turned. Over and over the men paced on a seven-hundred-foot walk, paying out the fibers with each hand as they paced. It was a dull task, but chanting made it more cheerful.

Tam listened to them, and she knew exactly what they were doing, for she had watched them ever since she was a tiny tot. Tam began to sway from the strain of holding herself in one position so long. The chanting began to sound more like a bee buzzing in her ears. The box of dates was heavier. Her neck had a crick in it. Her nose itched like mad. She did not dare to scratch it. Suddenly she sneezed so violently that she dropped the box of dates. Tam was terrified. She remembered Mr. Carter's temper when he was mad at Jeff's hat.

Moses Carter threw his stick of charcoal on the table. "That's all," he muttered. "Pick up that box and don't bother me any more." He directed the last remark to Jeff.

Tam looked at Jeff. He winked one eye at her, so Tam knew that Moses Carter wasn't as cranky as he sounded. She held out the box of dates to him. "Have some," she invited.

Absent-mindedly the wood carver took a handful and started munching them. Tam managed to get a peek at the drawing. It was startling to her, for only her curls and her chin were finished. All the rest of her face was indicated by a few scrawls.

"What are you going to do with this?" she asked.

"Huh?" Moses Carter grunted.

Tam repeated her question and added, "Why didn't you draw a nose and mouth? I have them on my face."

43

Moses Carter cackled, "I know you have, but what I want is the way your curls spring out from your head and the shape of your firm round chin."

He dashed to the chunk of elm wood and began making chalk marks on it where he would begin to chip away the wood. He forgot all about the children.

Jeff tugged at Tam's elbow. "Come, let's get out of here," he whispered.

At the back of the building the grass ended in a wooden embankment. There was water rippling in on the tide to fill the creek. The children stared out at the spars in the harbor. One ship had its sails all spread to catch the wind.

"I'm going to sea when I'm twelve," Jeff said.

Tam declared, "I'm going to dress like a boy and stow away until the ship is out too far for the captain to send me ashore."

Jeff laughed, then said, "Maybe you could fool them. You are strong and you could cut your hair shorter. Nobody would think you were a girl with all those freckles on your face."

Tam bragged, "I keep cutting my hair so it can't grow long, and I'm going to get stronger and stronger muscles."

A shrill voice broke into their plans for the future.

"Jeff! Jefferson Carter!"

"Ma wants me," Jeff said. At once he turned to go to the back door. Tam followed him. Mrs. Carter said, "I want you to run down to Debbie Salt-marsh's shop and buy a spool of thread."

"Oh, Ma," Jeff protested. "I'm not going to go in a ladies' shop and ask for a spool of thread. Why can't Prudence do it?"

Tam had followed Jeff into the big kitchen. Prudence was sitting at the window to catch the last rays of sunshine. She had an enormous skirt spread over her lap and was hemming it with flying fingers. Tam watched the flashing glint of her silver thimble and remembered back four or five years when her mother used to sit and sew just like Prue.

Prudence was older than Jeff. She was a young lady. "Oh, Jeff," she begged, never raising her eyes from the endless hem, "please get me some more thread. I want to wear this frock to the Reverend Bentley's singing school tonight. I want to look as stylish as that stuck-up Unity Parker."

Jeff groaned, "All right. Give me the money. Come on, Tam."

Tam held onto her box of dates and galloped beside Jeff down a narrow lane and into all the short cuts Jeff knew until they reached Main Street.

"Hark!" Jeff brought up short. "The town crier is coming along. I hear his bell. Let's wait and hear what the news is."

Tam and Jeff waited at the corner of Main Street and St. Peter Street. A tall, thin old man with spectacles perched on his long nose was ringing his large hand bell. Groups of children and grownups gathered around him. He read from a paper: " 'TO THE CURIOUS. To be seen at Mr. Benjamin Daland's near the town pump, Salem. TWO CAMELS, male and female, imported from Arabia. These stupendous Animals are most deserving the attention of the curious, being the greatest natural curiosity ever exhibited to the publick on this continent. They are 19 hands high—have necks near 4 feet long—have a large bunch on their backs, and another under their breasts, in the form of a pedestal, on which they support themselves when lying down. They have 4 joints in their hind legs and will travel 12 or 14 days without drinking, and carry a burthen of 1500 wt. They are remarkably harmless and docile and will lie down and rise at command.' "

The town crier then read a passage from Genesis about camels. He added after that, " 'The CAMELS will go from this town tomorrow evening.' "

Tam and Jeff milled around with the other children, chattering about the camels. One by one they started to run home to tell the amazing tale. Jeff was in a dream. "I'll see all sorts of strange animals when I go to sea."

Then Tam heard the bells ringing for the end of the working day. Shops were closing. "Jeff, you must get the thread right off," she warned.

He came to life with a start and ran across the street, dodging between horses and carriages and wagons, with Tam right after him.

The shop was closed. Jeff pounded on the door. "Open up, open up!" he yelled. Tam screamed, "Open up!"

People going by stopped to laugh at the frantic children.

Finally from an upper window a head poked out. "Shop is closed. Can't you see?" scolded a prim voice. "Go away and stop that horrible screaming or I'll call the constable."

Jeff shouted up to the head in the window, "Please, please open up so Prudence can wear her new frock."

Tam added her plea, "She aims to look smarter than that stuck-up Unity Parker."

The head withdrew. In a few minutes the door opened. Debbie Saltmarsh whispered, "I'd never

47

come down if you had not mentioned that Unity Parker. She turns up her nose at my goods and buys from the Frenchman's shop down the street where it's more fashionable."

Tam watched the tall skinny woman fumble around her wares. The shop smelled of wet cotton umbrellas and musty cellar smells and ancient dry attic timbers. There were ribbons and laces and needles and pins and strong-smelling cheap calico. Miss Saltmarsh wore a beribboned lavender cap over her false black frizz.

Jeff thanked her heartily and slammed the door after him. It was dark outdoors. The old lamp-lighter was going around with his ladder to light the smelly whale-oil lamps. Without a word Tam ran beside him. They burst into the kitchen, and Jeff panted, "Here it is."

Prudence was sewing by the light of a Betty lamp. She lifted her face and smiled. "You are a good boy, Jeff. Thank you so much."

Mrs. Carter was busy stirring up a kettle of salt fish, beets, and potatoes. She turned her flushed face from the hot fire and said, "Supper is nearly ready, Jeff. Don't go away. Call your father to come in."

Tam stood uncertainly in the doorway. She was reminded sharply of her own hearth, where no

supper was stewing for a hungry man. "I must go,"
she cried. "Good-by, Jeff." Then she turned back
before she closed the door. "See you at the town
pump tomorrow," she said.

When Tam reached the little house in Browne's Lane, there were no lamps or candles lighted. She couldn't figure out why her father wasn't home. A neighbor called, "Tam, your father left word that he was going to eat supper at the Cat and Wheel and he won't be home till late."

Tam stood at the door, bewildered. Her father was always home for supper and seldom went out in the evening. "Where did he go?" she cried out.

"Didn't say. Probably got tired of waiting around for his supper," was the jeering reply.

Tam lost her appetite. She didn't go into the house. She leaned on the fence, where wild cucumber vines climbed in a fragrant tangle. The creamy white flowers were like foam in the twilight. She loved their scent. Absent-mindedly she pinched the fat green seed pods that burst with a soft juicy pop and discharged their flat black seeds into her hand. She was sorry she had forgotten to come home early enough to cook a hot supper for her father. She felt lonesome, and before she knew it tears spurted from her eyes. She squeezed her eyes shut, but the tears came just the same. Angrily she rubbed her fists in her eyes. She hated crying girls. But it didn't help.

Sobs began to rise in her throat. She opened the door and blindly stumbled to her father's big chair. She curled up and cried noisily until she was exhausted. She fell asleep at last and did not wake until she felt strong arms lifting her out of the chair.

"Why aren't you in bed? It is much too late for you to be up." Her father's voice was tender.

Tam sighed, "I'm hungry." Then she was wide awake. "I'm sorry I wasn't home in time to cook your supper, Father."

She was standing at the hearth, rubbing the sleep out of her eyes. Her father was cutting a chunk of cold johnnycake and filling a mug with milk. "Here, Tam, eat this." He pushed her into a chair at the table.

"I guess I expect too much from a little girl. It's a

grown woman's work to cook and keep house," he said.

Tam wondered sleepily if her father was planning to hire a housekeeper. But she was too sleepy to think. She ate the last crumb of johnnycake and drained the mug and stumbled to her bed.

The next morning Tam spent cooking a fine chowder. She had gone down to the fisherman's wharf early to get a haddock for the chowder. She asked a neighbor how to make gingerbread, and she turned out a spicy-smelling slab of it. She made apple sauce and she stayed home until her father came in for dinner at noon.

"Why, lass, you are a pretty good cook," her father remarked.

Tam was uneasy. She didn't want to be known as a good cook. That was what other girls wanted to be praised for. She was torn between her duty to her father and her love of freedom and boyish ways. Tam changed the conversation. She told her father about the camels to be seen at the town pump. Her father said he'd never seen a camel.

"The camels will be here only until tonight," Tam said. "You could see them after supper."

Her father hemmed and hawed. "Well, I have other plans. I'm going out on business after supper and I won't be home till late."

Tam was dumfounded. "But, Father, you never go out on business after supper. I feel lonesome when you are away at night." Her voice was plaintive.

"I guess you'll have to grin and bear it," he said.

Tam eyed her father. He seemed to be feeling jolly. She couldn't understand what had happened to him. He rose from the table whistling "Up with the Bonnets of Bonnie Dundee." Then he was off and down the lane.

Tam washed the dishes and filled a kettle with meat and vegetables to simmer all afternoon over the fire. She went to buy a loaf of bread. So far she had not learned to bake bread. The woman who baked bread was kneading a new batch in a long wooden trough. Soft puffs of flour rose as she thumped the dough vigorously and cut it into loaves.

The bread already baked was taken from the huge brick oven and dumped out of the blackened tins onto a scrubbed and bleached pine table. It was a delicious-smelling kitchen. Tam put a crusty brown loaf in her basket and covered it with a clean towel. She put down her money and scampered off as fast as she could. She was impatient to be on her way to see the camels.

Tam took one quick look around the house, slammed the door, and tore down the lane, screeching at the top of her lungs because it was so good to be free from duties. She did not know how to let the good feeling out unless she screeched. The neighbors, as usual, shook their heads and said, "Whistling girls and crowing hens always come to bad ends."

Tam swung on the Carters' gate and yelled, "Jeff, Jeff—come out."

Jeff appeared from the back yard with a rake. "I have to finish raking leaves," he said.

Tam fumed, "Why do you rake up leaves when the wind will blow them away?"

Jeff said, "Ma is particular. I have to do this or else I can't go to see the camels."

Tam told him to hurry. She swung on the gate, and it squeaked and creaked so loudly that Mrs. Carter came to the door.

"Tam Morgan, you get right off that gate. You'll break the hinges and it won't close properly."

Tam slipped from the gate. Mrs. Carter shook a warning finger at her.

Then Tam climbed to the top of the fence and walked up and down, balancing herself and whistling at the same time.

Mrs. Carter came to the door again. "Tam Morgan, you'll fall and break your neck. Get off the fence this minute."

Tam leaped to the ground. Mrs. Carter continued, "Behave like a young lady." Then she banged the door shut.

Tam poked around the yard, waiting for Jeff. She bent to smell a rose, and all the petals fell apart and fluttered to the ground. She gave a quick glance at the door. Mrs. Carter did not appear to scold her. "I guess she didn't see me do that," Tam snickered.

Finally Jeff was ready to go. "I'll race you to the whipping post," he yelled. Down the lane they ran, turning into Church Street and then into School Street. Tam thought she would surely win the race, but Jeff sprinted ahead and touched the whipping post first. Panting and gasping for breath, they leaned against the post for a few minutes. Tam said, "Did you ever see anyone get whipped?"

"No," Jeff said, "but I heard about an apprentice who was bound out to a farmer and he ran away with his master's best coat, and when he was caught over in Danvers he was brought back and given a public whipping. That was only last week."

56

"Look at all the people going to see the camels," Tam cried. "Let's go."

The camels were in a roped-off enclosure. Tam and Jeff squirmed through the crowd and reached the rope. They were speechless with surprise. Neither had even seen a picture of a camel, and the huge humped creatures with their ragged coats were like nothing they had even imagined. Tam stared into the eyes of one camel, and she was awed by the haughty, disagreeable expression it had.

Jeff pinched his nose and muttered, "Phew, don't they stink!"

Tam giggled. "Maybe you smell the flakes." She pointed to the flake yard, where rows of codfish were drying in the sun. They were spread out on boards raised a few feet from the ground. It was a strong smell, but people living along the water front were used to the smell and rather liked it.

The man exhibiting the camels gave them orders and they would lie down, folding up their many joints, and when given an order to rise they would get up with a rocking motion. Tam noticed a woman going around with a hat collecting money. She realized that people were supposed to pay for the exhibition.

"Jeff," she whispered, "have you got any money?"

58

"No," he whispered back.

"I haven't either. Let's go away." Tam pushed herself under elbows and bumped into gawking people until she stood on the outskirts of the crowd. Jeff joined her. They sat on a rail fence and watched the people. "Look at the fat man." Tam laughed. "He dropped his money and he is too fat to bend over and pick it up." She screeched with glee.

But Jeff was not paying any attention to her. Tam turned her head. Jeff was gazing at a girl who was walking delicately over the rough field. A tall gentleman held her hand. She wore lace mitts halfway up to her elbows.

"Jeff." Tam nudged him. "There is Captain Cromwell."

Jeff was silent. Tam stole a quick glance at him. His face was bright with pleasure. She had never seen such a look of admiration on his face before. In fact, he acted as if he were unable to speak. She saw him slip down from the fence and slowly follow the captain. When they stopped to look at the crowd around the camels, Jeff edged in so he could continue to gaze at the girl. Tam had never seen a girl dressed so pretty. She had a leghorn hat tied with broad white ribbons under her chin, and flowers trimmed the brim. They were artificial flowers that looked just like the real ones. The girl stepped lightly in black slippers tied around her ankles, and her long skirts were of some light material sprigged with blue and pink flowers. She had a way of switching her skirts that fascinated Tam.

Tam got down from the fence and tried to wiggle her bottom to see what it would do to her skirt. But no amount of twisting and craning her neck would show her what the result was.

"Oh, pooh, I'm not going to act like that girl. She's silly," Tam muttered. But no matter what Tam told herself, she could not help sneaking up close to get a good look at the girl who had Jeff acting so queer.

Tam was so busy edging around that she didn't notice that Captain Cromwell was looking at her with a smile. He said, "Good afternoon, Mistress Morgan." It was a teasing voice. Tam lifted her face and blushed, much to her annoyance. She bobbed her head politely and stood still, not knowing how to open her mouth to speak the proper words of greeting. Captain Cromwell was amused at her embarrassment.

He said, "Tam, this is my daughter Felicity, who is just about your age."

Tam looked square at Felicity and saw that she was interested only in Jeff's bashful stare. But she turned to Tam and said, "It is a pleasure to make your acquaintance, Mistress Morgan." Her voice was cool and light, and Tam thought she sounded very grown up. Tam did not know what to do now, so she bobbed her head and tried to remember how her mother had taught her to curtsy long ago. She decided not to attempt it.

"Who is this lad?" Captain Cromwell asked when he saw Jeff come to Tam and nudge her elbow. The captain was away on so many long trips that he did not know children who had grown up while he was away.

"Jefferson Carter," Tam said.

Jeff bowed and spoke the proper words as if he had no shyness. He even asked Felicity what she thought of the camels.

"I have not seen them close up," she told him.

"I'll take you," Jeff said promptly, and he reached out and clasped her hand covered with a lace mitt, and gently led her to the ropes where she could look at the camels.

Tam's eyes followed them. This was the most astonishing experience she had ever had. Jeff, who said he hated prissy girls, was acting as if some witch had put a spell on him.

"Well, Tam," Captain Cromwell said, hunting

around for something to say, "I suppose you will be glad to go back to school in October?"

Tam scuffed her bare feet in the dusty earth. "I don't go to school. My father says girls don't need schooling. They should learn to cook and sew and take care of babies."

Captain Cromwell said sternly, "That is old-fashioned. I'm surprised a man of your father's intelligence should cherish notions of that sort. I'll speak to him. You must learn to read and write and do numbers."

Tam was horrified. She could read a few simple words and write a few words and do numbers on her fingers. Her father had taught her that much. Now Captain Cromwell was going to manage it so that her freedom would be taken from her and she would have to sit on a hard bench all day long in a stuffy room. She looked so downcast that Captain Cromwell put his hands in his pockets and jingled his coins. The woman with the hat was coming toward them. "Here, Tam, give her a penny." He handed Tam a penny, and she dropped it in the hat. The captain put in a handful of coins.

Then he left to get his daughter. When he came back he said, "I'll bring Felicity to see how the ship is progressing. She ought to know that ship from the very beginning until it is launched."

Felicity looked at Jeff. "I am going to christen the ship," she said proudly.

Tam's heart leaped up and bumped furiously in her breast. That girl was going to christen the ship Tam's father was building. A girl—and her father had said that girls never christened ships. Tam's voice came out in a squeaking question: "What is to be the name of the ship?"

She felt as if she was back in her dream. She just had to know the name. The name of the ship was important to her. She felt jealous to think that Felicity should have an interest in the ship. After all, it was Tam who collected wood for treenails and who watched the brig being built. But Felicity shook her head. "I don't know." She looked up at her father. His steely eyes were fond and gentle. "I don't either, Felicity. Not until the day of the christening will that name be spoken aloud."

Tam sighed. If she could only remember her dream. She was sure she had spoken the name and her father had wakened her too soon and broken off the dream. Tam was determined to dream that dream again and remember what name she gave to the brig when it felt life along its keel and slid into the water.

Captain Cromwell took Felicity by the hand. They said good-by, and Felicity smiled sweetly at

Jeff and Tam before they went down School Street. Jeff watched until they were out of sight. Then he drew a long breath, as if he had come up from a deep dive.

"Where does she live?" He spoke softly, as if even to speak of Felicity was a delight.

Tam answered in a tempery voice, "She lives with her father."

Jeff continued in the same way, "Where does he live?"

Tam snapped out, "He built a house 'way out on Main Street. You'll never get invited there."

Jeff merely said, "Humph, you won't either."

Tam's temper rose like a flood, and before she knew it she was punching and kicking Jeff with all her might. She didn't know why she was so angry at him except that she had a strange, unfamiliar ache in her heart. Jeff gave her a hard shove, and she sat down in the dirt. "You're a jealous pig," he yelled, and went off, leaving her sitting in the dust.

Slowly she got up and wandered moodily through the town. She looked in the shopwindows but took no notice of what she saw. How often she and Jeff had looked in the shopwindows, taking turns at choosing what they wanted if they had money to spend. She heard the town crier coming down the street. He stopped near her and

read from his paper about a runaway Negro man named Cato. He described the man's clothes and said that two dollars reward would be given for his return.

Tam was tempted to run away at once and be a stowaway on a ship. Then she could imagine the town crier announcing her disappearance. She could almost see her father frantic and sad because Tam had left him with no one to see that the lamps were lit when he came home from the shipyard. It was so real that her throat hurt with choked-down sobs. Without a moment's hesitation she flew home to assure her grieving father that she had not really run away.

By the time Tam reached home she was over her imaginary flight from Salem. She lit the lamps and candles and stirred up the fire. Her father came in soon, and they sat down to eat supper. Thomas Morgan said, "Don't forget to put the beans on to soak tonight. Tomorrow is Saturday, you know." Tam was apt to forget what day of the the week it was.

"Father," Tam spoke up, "the bread woman bakes beans and brown bread for people. She says it is old-fashioned to bake your own beans. I see people come to her house on Saturdays, and they carry away beans and brown bread in their bundle handkerchiefs."

"Yes, I know." her father broke in. "They are

the same people who belong to the Social Library. They carry home books in their bundle handkerchiefs. They spend so much time reading and talking by the hour about books that they neglect their duties at home."

"People like Captain Cromwell?" Tam asked.

Her father shook his head. He never had a fault to find with his employer. Thomas Morgan had his mouth full of gingerbread. He had no more to say, and he ate rapidly and left the table in a rush. Before Tam could tell him about Felicity Cromwell and the astonishing news that she was going to christen the ship, Thomas Morgan was squinting at himself in the wavy mirror. He combed his back hair and clubbed it into a dark blue silk bag and tied it firmly. Tam giggled. She thought her father's hair was like a horse's tail with a ribbon on it. He put on his hat and called from the door, "Put the beans on to soak, lass, then go to bed."

There was an empty feeling in the house without her father's deep voice with the rough Scottish burr in it. Tam washed the dishes, picked over the beans, and put them in a kettle of water to soak overnight. She was listless. She dawdled over placing the pewter plates on the dresser shelves. She noticed the cover of her box of dates was half off. She looked in, wondering if she felt like eating a date. To her surprise, the box was almost empty. She was puzzled. Her father said he didn't care much for dates, and Tam herself had not eaten more than two or three since she brought the box home.

What had happened to them? Suddenly she seemed to see her father going out the door, and now she remembered how one pocket bulged and stuck out.

"I wonder if Father took some dates with him?" she mused. "Why would he take dates to a meeting of carpenters? Where did he go?"

Tam was baffled. It was a complete mystery to her. She yawned widely. The washbowl was filled with water, and she splashed her face and hands in the soapy water, not caring about the backs of her ears or her wrists. She threw the bowl of water out the back door, undressed, and got into her long cotton nightgown. She tied on her nightcap and climbed into bed. "Now I'm going to dream." She pulled the quilt up under her chin. "I'm going to dream and not wake up until I say the name of the ship . . . the name of the ship . . ." She was sound asleep. She had no dreams.

Saturday morning Tam had to be wakened by her father.

69

"Coom, lass, I'm late myself in waking. I can't wait for you to cook breakfast, so I'll just eat some cold food and be off."

Tam slid out of bed. The sun was shining in her window through the branches of a tree, making bright patterns on the floor. She was eager to be out of doors, but her father's last words were, "Put the beans on. I built up the fire."

Tam spent the morning cooking and cleaning the house. Tomorrow would be Sunday, when no cooking was done—that is, nothing but tea or some light dish was prepared. It was a day of churchgoing and reading the Bible.

There was money in the old tin canister to buy food. Tam shopped dutifully and staggered home with a loaded basket. She had dinner ready for her father at noon. He was full of the news that Captain Cromwell expected one of his ships in at any hour. Tam was excited. That meant Jeff would be on the wharf. The boy who first sighted the ship would be given fifty cents. Thomas Morgan knew just how Tam felt. In fact, all Salem was agog.

Tam joined the people milling around on Cromwell's Wharf. There she found Jeff yelling and struggling to be the first to spy the sails of the ship. Tam scrambled up a rickety outside stairway to the upper floors of a sail loft. Jeff knew she had sharp

eyes and would give him a signal so he would be the first to cry out the name of the ship to the clerk in the countinghouse.

Jeff squinted up at Tam, who was clinging like a monkey to the topmost railing. She let go her hold with one hand and made a quick motion. Jeff strained his eyes. Yes, he saw a faint blur on the horizon as Tam had indicated. He dashed to the door of the countinghouse and yelled, "The *Mercury!*"

Other boys screamed and jumped up and down with the ringing cry, "The *Mercury!* The *Mercury!*"

But it was granted that Jeff had been the first to yell the ship's name, and he was given fifty cents.

Everybody else was yelling now, for the *Mercury* was in Salem Harbor, and bells began to ring, announcing her arrival. Tam climbed down from her perch and yelled, "Hurrah! Hurrah!" She bumped into the collector of customs hustling down the wharf to the customs boat. He stepped on her bare toes with his heavy shoes. She didn't feel any pain because she was dizzy with the fever and commotion that were bringing more and more people to the wharf. It was a glorious sight to those living in Salem to see the ship standing out there with the harbor master's sloop bounding over the waves to meet her and give her anchorage.

Captain Cromwell was ready to greet the skipper of his ship. Tam and Jeff worked their way through the crowd to stand near him. They saw the longboat put off from the *Mercury*. Soon the skipper was shaking hands with Captain Cromwell and going with him into the countinghouse to give a report of his long voyage.

Tam eyed the sailors in the longboat. Dressed for shore leave, they wore blue and white jerseys, short roundabout jackets, flaring trousers, varnished black shoes, and varnished black hats with dangling ribbons.

"Look!" Tam clutched Jeff's arm. "One of the sailors has a little monkey sitting on his shoulder, and the monkey has his tail around the sailor's neck. Oh, I wish I had a little monkey too."

"I'll bring you a monkey when I come home from a voyage," Jeff promised.

The sailors came up from the boat, sun-browned husky young men who rolled along the wharf. They were followed by girls and boys admiring and asking questions. The sailors made their way to the nearest tavern. Derby Street was loud with chatter and the bustle of merchants. Laughing girls exclaimed over the gold earrings the sailors wore and shrank from the weird designs on the sailors' hands and wrists that had been done in India ink in some faraway Eastern seaport.

In no time there were music and singing and drinking and eating in all the taverns. With many other children Tam and Jeff hung around with eyes popping and ears open to every tale of adventure. Tam was boiling over with high spirits. The children were not allowed to come into the tavern, but when the music of a hornpipe reached her, Tam began to dance. The children made a circle around her. She hopped and kicked with such vigor that some of the sailors came to the tavern door to add their cheers. Tam tossed her brilliant red curls and grinned from ear to ear. She did not hear a shocked voice call "Tamesine!" Not until her father clapped a firm hand on her shoulder did she know that he was present.

"Stop these monkeyshines at once." His voice was stern and cold. His hand drew her out of the crowd of snickering children and laughing grown-ups.

Jeff followed until Thomas Morgan had his daughter in the shipyard. He could see that Mr. Morgan's face was as dark as a thundercloud. He did not follow them into the shed. He waited until Tam's howls of anguish had let up. Thomas Mor-

74

gan came out, followed by Tam rubbing herself where she had been spanked.

"Go right home," her father ordered.

Tam blubbered and started off toward Browne's Lane. Jeff came up to her.

"Tam, I'll buy you some candy with part of my prize money."

Tam sniffed, "I don't want any candy."

"Aw, Tam, what do you want?" Jeff wheedled.

"I want to run away to sea and never come back again, and then my father would be sorry he was so mean to me," she sputtered with temper.

"But, Tam, girls shouldn't run away to sea. They have to stay home and wear pretty frocks and hats with ribbons." Jeff tried to comfort her.

Tam swung around and looked at Jeff. "You mean like Felicity Cromwell?" Her voice rose in a pained cry. Jeff, who had always thought Tam the perfect companion in every way, was changing. There was no doubt of that. Ever since he had seen Felicity he had been acting differently.

Jeff smiled and nodded. "You would look pretty, too, Tam, if you were cleaner and wore a hat so you wouldn't get all those freckles on your face."

Tam's face showed a battle of conflicting thoughts. First she wondered if she could look like

75

Felicity, then when she thought of wearing a hat and shoes and perhaps those silly lace mitts, she got mad all over again. Added to that was the fact that Felicity was going to christen the brig. "I hate you, Jeff Carter. I'm never going to speak to you again."

Tam turned to run the rest of the way in the lane and into the house. She peeked through the window. Jeff went by without coming in to ask her to make up and be friends again as he usually did when they had a squabble.

Tam sulked until her father came in. "Have you filled up the big kettles with water?" he asked.

Tam shook her head. Her father went about lugging in water from a neighboring well. The water was to be heated for their Saturday-night baths.

Tam set out the smoking hot baked beans and brown bread. The steam from them curled up and smelled good of molasses and pork. They ate supper silently, each busy with his own thoughts.

After a big bowl of apple sauce Thomas Morgan said, "I want you to scrub thoroughly, Daughter, and wash your hair too. After church tomorrow we are going to Marblehead."

Tam's sulky face broke into a smile. "To see Nathaniel and wee Jamie! I declare, I almost forgot about them. It is a long time between visits."

76

Thomas Morgan said, "Aye, it is too long between visits. The boys may not remember their sister."

Tam began to perk up. She washed the dishes and laid out the clean clothes she would wear on Sunday. Her father filled the wooden washtub with hot and cold water until Tam said it was just right. The tub was placed near the fire. Thomas Morgan went to his room to lay out his Sunday clothes and a clean nightshirt and nightcap. He would take his bath after Tam was in bed.

Tam splashed and scrubbed and ducked her dripping curls time and again in the soapy water. She came out of the tub pink and glowing. Her feet looked so clean that she eyed them with a giggle. "They are as pink as suckling pigs," she thought.

The big coarse towel dried her in a jiffy, and she rubbed her sopping hair until it stood up in a soft red halo. The fireplace sent out enough heat to dry her hair quickly. She slipped into her nightgown and called, "I'm all clean, Father. You can empty the tub now."

Bed was cozy and sleep came almost at once. Thomas Morgan took one look at her clean face and fluffy hair spread out on the pillow. She had forgotten to put on her nightcap. He thought earnestly about his plans for her future and he wondered if Tam was going to be difficult to manage. He picked up the tub of water and threw it out the kitchen door. Then he filled it with hot water for his bath. He was very thoughtful and sober. When he was ready for bed, he kneeled down and prayed solemnly and long for the Lord's guidance.

Tam put on her Sunday-go-to-meeting clothes. She groaned when she stood up in her shoes. Wearing shoes only on Sunday was punishment for her feet. "They pinch my toes," she grumbled to herself. She didn't like wearing stockings any better. Her father called from the next room, "Hurry, lass, I hear the first bell."

Tam's dress buttoned in back, and she squirmed around trying to reach the middle button, but she couldn't, so she gave up trying. Her curls sprang up in wild confusion. No amount of combing would tame them. She jammed on her bonnet and tied the worn strings under her chin.

"Lass, come noo. 'Tis time to leave for the kirk."

Tam began to smile. Her father was feeling

good when he used so many Scottish words. As soon as church was over and dinner eaten they would start for Marblehead, and that meant they would not go to the second service in the afternoon. She clumped noisily into the kitchen. Her father wore his best long-skirted coat. The breeches had silver buckles at the knee, and his shoes had silver buckles also.

"You have a new hat, Father!" Tam cried. "It doesn't turn up as much as your old one."

"This is the latest fashion," he explained, and set the cocked hat on his head.

Tam was surprised. Her father had never before shown any interest in what might be the latest fashion.

The second bell was ringing. Tam and her father walked sedately along Main Street. Families of children, headed by father and mother arm in arm, walked demurely behind. There was a Sabbath hush on the street. The East Meeting House was crowded. Each square pew was fully occupied. Tam saw Dr. Bentley appear from a small door under the high pulpit. A double staircase led to the pulpit, and he bustled up one in his flowing black gown and faced the congregation.

Tam liked his pleasant round face. It was a friendly face. The singing of hymns, the long

sermon, the prayers offered for fathers and sons at sea were given in a serious voice that boomed out from under the sounding board. He gave thanks for the safe delivery of two babies born during the past week. Tam thought the Lord must be very busy looking after the men far away at sea who had not been heard of for a year or two. All through the service she wiggled and yawned and kicked her restless heels on the back of the pew, until her father put his large hand on her knee and shook his head at her. She sighed. She felt hungry, and her stomach made little growling noises. She itched all over. Finally the benediction was pronounced, and Tam sprang to unfasten the pew door.

The September air was good and sweet after the dry churchy smell that Tam had been breathing for hours. She left like running, but her father was greeting friends and exchanging news with other men. He held her hand firmly, knowing how skittish Tam was feeling.

Dinner was eaten quickly, and Tam tied an apron over her best frock to wash the dishes. Her father went out, saying he would be back in a few minutes. When he returned, Tam was amazed. He was riding a horse from the livery stable. He hitched it to the fence and came in smiling. "Are you ready noo?"

Tam squealed with delight. "You have a horse! We are going to ride. I thought we would have to walk."

She yanked on her bonnet, and in a jiffy she was out of the house and on the horse with her arms around her father's waist. The horse trotted through Main Street until they reached the highway to Marblehead. They crossed over the Mill Dam, where Daniel Malloon's granary and mill were silent and deserted. The horse took them through South Salem and into the sandy wagon road. Tam twisted her head this way and that to take in the sights. Now she saw sheep pastures, with bells on the sheep tinkling lightly in the soft air. Salt marshes spread on either side as they rode on. Then came clumps of willows and the town began to appear.

Tam's visits to Marblehead had been so long ago that she hardly remembered the narrow twisting streets and the lopsided huddled houses. Thomas Morgan stopped in front of one house. He dismounted, and Tam leaped to the ground, disdaining his helping hand. He tied the horse to a hitching post. Tam was excited. She wondered if the boys would know her. Thomas Morgan lifted the knocker, and the door opened. Aunt Tabby greeted them. "I declare, Tamesine, you have grown to be a big girl. Come in, come in." She led the way to the parlor, which was opened only for company.

"Where are the boys?" Thomas Morgan asked. Before he could be answered two small boys came running into the parlor and flung themselves around his legs.

"They know you," Tam said, "but they don't know me."

Aunt Tabby gave a choked snicker. "They have been seeing their father quite often lately."

Tam eyed her father with curiosity. "You didn't tell me you had been here." She was grieved.

"Well——" her father hemmed and hawed. His face grew red. "Well——" he started again, and stopped, as if he did not know how to go on.

"For pity's sake, Thomas Morgan, come out with it," Aunt Tabby snapped.

Tam looked from one to the other. Something mysterious was going on between them. Thomas Morgan sat down in a chair and said, "Come here, Daughter."

She leaned against him. He put his arm around her waist. The boys hung on his knees. "I have been calling on a lady who lives nearby. She is going to be my wife—and your mother."

Tam grew stiff as a rod of iron. Her father

84

swallowed nervously. "And the boys will have a home with us too. Doesn't that sound fine to you, lass?"

Tam did not say a word. He hugged her harder and shook her a little. "Tam?" His voice was so loving that Tam's heart ached. But the thought of a strange woman in their little house was more than she could bear. To her horror, she began to sob. She pushed her face into her father's shoulder. The rough cloth and the good clean smell that always clung to him made her cry harder.

Aunt Tabby said, "Give her time to get used to the idea, Thomas. Tell her that now she won't have to keep house and that she can go to school."

Tam raised a woebegone face from her father's shoulder. "School?" she blubbered. "I don't want to go to school." Her voice went up in a wail of despair.

The boys were puzzled. They started to cry too.

"Oh, my lands!" Aunt Tabby cried. "Such goings on. Thomas Morgan, you go to call on Abigail and let me handle these young ones."

Thomas Morgan rose from the chair and went quickly to the door.

"Now then," Aunt Tabby began, "it ain't fitting that a child like you should have so much responsibility. You'll be an old woman long before your time. And it ain't fitting that a busy, hard-working man like your father should have to give so much of his time to housekeeping and bringing up a daughter. It stands to reason that your father should marry again. He is a young man. And then he could have the boys, who need a father's hand to bring them up—yes, and to tan their backsides too."

Tam lifted a tear-stained face to Aunt Tabby, who was nervously pleating her Sunday white muslin apron between her fingers. She could see that Aunt Tabby was trying her best to help Tam get used to the change that was going to take place in the small house in Browne's Lane.

"Have you seen—her?" Tam gulped out.

"Of course. Didn't I pick Abigail Wiggins for your father? Didn't I send for him to come prancing over here because one of the boys was poorly? And may the Lord forgive me, the boy was full of health."

Tam sat up straight. So this was where her father had been on the nights when he said he had to be out on business. So this was the reason her father had been sprucing up, even to buying a new hat. It was to Abigail that he had given some of Tam's dates. He had been courting that woman, Abigail Wiggins.

Tam could just see how a woman with that name would look. She'd have a long hooked nose and a thin mouth that shut like a trap. She would be tall and skinny, and she would give Tam so many orders that there would not be enough time to carry them out, and after that Tam would be punished. Perhaps she would be whipped with a rod and not by her father's big gentle hand. Tam's lips trembled. It was all too dreadful to think about. She would certainly chop off her hair and borrow Jeff's clothes and stow away on the first ship that left Salem.

Tam let out howl after howl of sorrow. The boys looked at her for a moment in wonder, and then they crawled into the chair with her and added their howls to hers. Aunt Tabby scolded, "Stop it at once. The house sounds like Bedlam. I can't stand such an ungodly racket, and on the Sabbath too."

She turned away to hide her face in the window curtains, trying not to add her sobs to those of the unhappy children. Just then she saw Thomas Morgan with Abigail and thought it was high time they took over the family.

"Tam, my dear child, dry your tears. Here comes your father, and he has Abigail with him."

Tam leaped up in consternation. The boys sprawled on the floor. "No! No! I won't see her. I won't!" She flew to the back of the house and hid in the pie closet.

During the winter the pie closet was always filled with pies. They kept well because they froze in the unheated closet. But in September there was only half a blueberry pie and the remains of an apple pandowdy up high enough so the small boys could not reach them. Now that Tam had slammed the door shut, she could not see a thing in the dark cubbyhole.

She leaned against the door. She burrowed her head in her arms and tried to stop crying. At last the sobs that had been tearing her throat died away. The fragrance of the blueberry pie and the whiff of cinnamon and molasses from the apple pandowdy began to tease her nose. She turned around and fumbled for the pie. She felt one cut triangle of pie, and even if it was dripping with juice she managed to transfer it to her mouth. The blueberries made her think of the hot summer days when she and Jeff picked blueberries and sold them for a few pennies to the rich folks who lived in the big houses on Main Street. They would go to the back door and loiter long enough to admire the fancy little summerhouses and the handsome gardens before the cook came to the door to buy the berries.

Tam thought of Jeff and his admiration for Felicity Cromwell, who lived in a big house. "She is a stuck-up girl, and Jeff won't have any fun with her even if she does invite him to her house," Tam said to herself. "I hate her. It isn't fair that she should christen the brig my father is building."

She decided to leave the pie closet and slip out the back door and go home by herself. But there was no way to open the door from the inside. A latch had clicked shut on the other side of the door, and she was a prisoner.

Tam kicked the door and banged her fists on it, but no one came to let her out. "Aunt Tabby!" she yelled. But there wasn't a sound from the kitchen. She called again and again. Sometimes she called, "Father!" Still no one came to let her out. She screamed with temper finally and kicked and pounded the door until the latch rattled, but it did not open the door. "They have left me to die," she panted.

Furiously she grabbed for the pie and dashed it to the floor. The apple pandowdy followed. She stamped on them. She would get even with Aunt Tabby for being so cruel to her. Finally Tam sank

to the floor and leaned against the door. Her knees felt wobbly and her throat hurt from so much screeching. Her voice was only a hoarse croak. "Let me out—let me out."

Then the door opened and Tam pitched forward. A horrified gasp went up from Aunt Tabby. "The poor child was in here!"

Tam felt herself being sat up on the floor. A hand brushed back her tumbled curls and a stranger's voice said, "Poor little lamb."

Tam's eyes blinked. She had been in the dark so long that she was blinded by the sunlight pouring in the open kitchen door. She saw her father and her small brothers come in and stand stunned at the sight of her on the floor.

Tam looked at the face close to hers. It was that of a stranger. It was a rosy dimpled face with light brown curls at each side. A puffy white muslin cap crowned the head of this stranger. Tam heard Aunt Tabby say, "She is stained with blueberry juice from top to toe."

Nathaniel poked around the closet. "She ate the pie!" he accused. Wee Jamie pushed into the closet. "She ate the pudding!" he cried. He shook a finger at Tam. "You are a naughty girl." he declared, sounding as much like Aunt Tabby as he could.

"No, no, Jamie. Tam isn't a naughty girl," the strange young woman said. She lifted Tam to a standing position with her strong arms. "Get a basin of water, Thomas," she said. Aunt Tabby broke in, "I'll get a towel."

Tam found herself being washed and fussed over by both women. They found blueberries in her hair and on her dress and on her shoes. Aunt Tabby said, "There now, Abigail, I guess we've done all we can to make her presentable."

Tam's eye popped wide open. This young woman certainly did not look like the Abigail Wiggins she had pictured in her mind. Tam finally spoke. She was feeling better, and her throat had stopped hurting. She managed a husky "Thank you, ma'am."

"There now," Aunt Tabby said, "that's the girl."

Tam's mouth curled in a smile. She couldn't help it. Abigail kissed her firmly on her clean cheek. It had been a long time since any woman had kissed Tam. It was nice to be kissed. Abigail seemed to know how Tam was feeling, and she kissed the other cheek.

Nathaniel pressed close. "Kiss me too," he demanded. Jamie, always his brother's shadow and imitator, put up his face for a kiss.

Nathaniel said, "We thought you were outdoors and we hunted for you. We hunted in all the places where Jamie and I always hide from Aunt Tabby."

Tam grinned. She knew some good hiding places around Browne's Lane. Then it flashed on her that she could show those places to her brothers because they would be living with her and their father and—Tam knew it was coming—with their new mother.

A tight feeling around Tam's heart began to melt away, and something warm took its place. It was a pleasant feeling that rose up and made her bashfully lean against Abigail and made her put her arms around Abigail's waist.

Aunt Tabby stood there blowing her nose and pushing her Sunday cap this way and that. She was nervous as a witch, she told herself. This had been a Sunday afternoon she would not forget in a hurry.

Thomas Morgan had been sitting beside the table, drumming his fingers on the scrubbed board. He had never had such a fright in his life as when Tam was missing and they had scrambled over the rocks on the headlands, worrying for fear she had slipped on wet seaweed and been drowned. But here she was, looking a sight all stained with the purple juice, but taking to Abigail in a way that warmed his heart and made him impatient to bring his bride home. The banns had been announced in the Marblehead church, and in a week he would come again to be married to Abigail.

During the week Thomas Morgan fixed a room under the eaves for Tam. "We'll put the boys in your room," he told her.

She brushed the cobwebs from a small window in a gable and looked out. "I can see 'way over the harbor. There are four ships standing there. I see one raising its sails, but it is only a schooner." Tam turned to her father. He was measuring the attic room and jotting down notes.

"I'll have to have some plastering done here before winter or it will be too cold for you. A partition on the other side of the chimney will give us an extra room." He was half talking to himself.

"Oh, Father, I thought I would have all the attic to myself." Tam frowned.

Her father said, "A family grows and needs more room."

"But we have enough rooms now," Tam insisted. "Enough for us all."

Her father pocketed his notes and picked up the measuring rod. He began whistling "Up with the Bonnets of Bonnie Dundee." He turned and said, "Come down, Tam, and bring up the bedding while I move the furniture."

They struggled up and down the steep narrow stairs many times before Tam's room was settled. Thomas Morgan planned to bring furniture from Aunt Tabby's house for the boys' room.

He washed his hands and sat down to the early supper Tam had ready. He had taken the afternoon off to change the house around.

"Coom, lass," he said when supper was over. "I'm going to see Mr. Carter about some scroll-work for the ship."

"Oh, Father," Tam cried, "then we can see the figurehead." She told him about her adventure with Mr. Carter as they walked along the lanes.

The September moon was standing white and full in the sky. There was a purple haze over the land. In the west great white clouds tinged with the last crimson of the setting sun were moving in a procession across the sky. Tam raised her head and stared steadily at the clouds.

"I see two lambs—I see—— It is an angel with spreading wings and, Father, I see God. He is so big!" She pointed up. Her voice fell. "He is gone."

Tam's voice was full of wonder. "Didn't you see Him?" she asked.

Thomas Morgan said no. "Only womenfolk see such things." Then he stopped and eyed Tam with interest. "Come to think of it, my grandmother Morgan could see things in the clouds and she could tell you what dreams meant and sometimes she could tell you what was going to happen long before anyone else." He shook his head. "Sad things that you'd rather not know until they happened. She had second sight, they said."

They were interrupted by Jeff's voice. He was down on his knees, clipping grass around his mother's flower beds.

"Hey!" he called.

Thomas Morgan opened the gate. "Is your father home, Jeff?" he asked.

Jeff leaped to his feet. "Yes, sir." He bobbed his head politely and led the way to the back door. They seldom used the front door.

Mr. Carter was sitting in a rocking chair with two black and white cats in his lap. He was eating

97

an apple and crunching through its skin with such gusto that spurts of juice sprang out in every direction.

"Draw up a chair," he invited.

Thomas Morgan settled down and helped himself to an apple from the wooden bowl. Tam heard Mrs. Carter and Prudence chattering in another room. She sat on the settle to wait for Jeff to finish his chores. The men talked awhile about the carved scrolls. Mr. Carter said it was too late to go to the workroom to see the figurehead. "I haven't got it far enough along to show you. Wait a few weeks," he said. Then the men began to talk about the latest news. Jeff came in. He took an apple and gave one to Tam. Their jaws moved steadily until they heard Thomas Morgan say, "On Thursday, October 29, President George Washington is coming to visit Salem."

The children stopped chewing. They got up from the settle and piped together, "General Washington!" as if they could not believe their ears.

General George Washington was every child's hero, and to think that such a great man, the greatest man in America, should come to Salem was enough to make them speechless at first.

"Hurrah! Hurrah!" they screeched. Jeff

punched Tam with enthusiasm. "There will be a parade," he cried.

Tam pushed Jeff vigorously, and he lost his balance and they rolled on the neatly sanded floor like two frolicking puppies. The cats in Mr. Carter's lap opened sleepy eyes and wondered if they should leave that warm cozy lap for a quieter room.

Mrs. Carter and Prue came running into the kitchen to see what the rumpus was about. They never knew what might happen when that wild Tam Morgan was around. But they added their chirps of amazement, and the kitchen was filled with excited questions and answers.

Thomas Morgan said that the ship carpenters would march in the parade with the sailmakers and the ropewalkers. He was saying, "We would like to have you lead the section, Mr. Carter. After all, the figureheads you carve to ornament the prows of our ships always breast the waves first."

Mr. Carter patted his cats so hard that they arched their backs and hissed angrily at him before they leaped to the floor. He was delighted to be so honored, and he called to his wife to fix a glass of flip for Thomas Morgan and himself. "To celebrate," he explained.

Tam and Jeff each took a cat, and they sat close

together on the settle, whispering. They were going to follow the procession along the whole route, and nobody was going to stop them.

The days went by as usual until a special day came that brought a hired chaise to the door to take them to Marblehead. It was the wedding day. Tam had her checked bundle handkerchief bulging with her everyday garments, for she was to spend a few days after the wedding visiting Aunt Tabby. She climbed into the chaise, whistling and yelling good-by to the neighbors. They shook their heads as they always did and said to each other, "Maybe the new Mistress Morgan will be able to tame that girl."

The wedding took place in the Wigginses' parlor. Tam saw that Abigail reached only to her father's shoulder. Aunt Tabby wept with such pleasure at the result of her matchmaking that her best cap slipped back on her head and gave her a tipsy appearance. The feast was spread; the guests ate and toasted the bride and groom. Tam and the boys left the crowded house and went to play on the headlands. When they came back, Tam discovered that her father and Abigail had already driven off in the chaise. Aunt Tabby said it was time for them to go home.

Tam felt sad. She had missed seeing her father go off in the chaise. She stared out the bedroom window toward Salem. Over the swaying masts she could see the gabled warehouses, tall and mysterious in the twilight. She knew so well the excitement of smelling strange cargoes from foreign lands. The scent of cassia packed in matted and plaited baskets, the sharpness of camphor cakes, the sting of pepper from Sumatra, ginger from India, and sacks of coffee from Arabia. Those warehouses breathed out so many conflicting

odors that only a child living in Salem could separate and identify each.

Tam longed to be back home. Marblehead had little to offer her. There were no milk-white Arabian horses coming off the ships with their Arabian grooms, to be presented to some Salem merchant as a gift from the Sultan of Muscat. There were no dark brown Spanish boys from the West Indies come to be educated in Salem. The treasures and people of many lands came to Salem.

Marblehead, Tam decided, was only a cluttered fishing village. Marblehead women sold fish in Salem markets, and they did not even seem to speak the same language. They had a dialect of their own. A few good families lived there. She remembered hearing that Aunt Tabby's folks and the Wiginses and some others she had seen at the wedding were fine old families. But there was only one place in the world where she wanted to be, and that was in Salem in a little house in Browne's Lane.

Aunt Tabby came into the room. "Tam, you go to bed now. Don't stand there mooning. I'm going to make piccalilli in the morning as long as you are here to help chop the vegetables."

That was enough to bring Tam sharply back to

everyday life. It reminded her that life in Salem was many times mixed with hateful duties such as cooking and cleaning.

Two days later Thomas Morgan came with a wagon to move the boys' furniture to Salem. Aunt Tabby cried when the boys left, mostly because she was glad to get rid of the responsibility. She promised to visit them in Salem.

When the wagon drew near home, Tam began to feel queer. Her stomach felt fluttery. It was going to be so different. She wanted to run down to the wharf and find her friend, Peg-leg Jeggles. But before she knew it, Abigail was in the doorway, laughing and welcoming her and the boys. "Tam," she said, "I can't wait to have you show me the brig your father is building."

Tam was surprised. Abigail didn't act like a stepmother. Tam was thoughtful. Then she burst out, "Do you want to see the figurehead Jeff's father is carving?"

Abigail beamed. "I'd admire to very much."

Then she got busy settling the boys' bedroom. Tam went up to her room under the eaves. She found a new patch quilt on the bed, a braided rug on the floor, and a new blue-and-white Canton water pitcher and bowl on the stand. The casement window sparkled. Not a cobweb was in sight. The dusty attic smell was gone.

Tam leaned out the window. It dawned on her that Abigail was a good housekeeper and that now she wouldn't have to think about housekeeping and cooking. A great load slipped from Tam's mind. "I'll be free." She laughed aloud and tore down the steps, out of the house, and into the lane, screeching with high spirits.

Tam strutted along to Main Street, whistling as loud as she could. When she reached the corner she almost ran into the good Dr. Bentley. He had a group of girls walking sedately two by two.

"Tamesine." He spoke with pleasure. "I am glad to see you and to tell you how happy I am that you have a mother. Do come along and I'll tell you about trees—that is our subject today."

"Trees," thought Tam to herself. "I know all about trees. I know more than he does."

Dr. Bentley went on: "It will be good for you to walk with these nice girls. You need girl friends."

Tam's saucy voice rang out, "I don't like girls. I don't want any girl friends." She turned away.

Then she caught sight of a long low cart being drawn by a pair of oxen. There was a load of barrels on it bound for some shipyard. Tam ran and jumped up among the barrels. She saw the shocked faces of the proper little girls and the look of dismay on Dr. Bentley's rosy round face. She felt rebellious. He was trying to take away her freedom. Tam stuck out her tongue at them and then she scrambled up to sit near the driver.

The next morning Tam was set on being very good. She did not tell Abigail about her meeting with Dr. Bentley the day before.

She took her stepmother and the two boys to inspect the brig. Tam found that Abigail did not know a thing about ships. She didn't know a broadax from an adze. She didn't know that the plankers, the highest-paid carpenters, were busy with the most exciting part of building a ship.

"Look!" Tam pointed. "There is the steam box. That's where the planks are softened." Tam's face was glowing. She loved shipbuilding.

They heard the plankers yell, "Hot plank!" Then the plankers hoisted the heavy, hot plank and rushed with it up an inclined plane to bend the plank around the curves of the stern of the growing brig. They did the same to the bow. The softened planks were forced tight against the frames and fastened by treenails. It took strong, husky men to do that work.

Tam announced proudly, "I gathered those trunnels in the woods."

Abigail was much impressed. "Why, Tam, I believe you are as much help to your father as a boy would be."

Tam grinned with delight. That was the nicest thing anyone could tell her. Nathaniel piped up, "I'm going to help Father when I am bigger."

Jamie echoed him, "I'm going to help Father when I am bigger too."

They were joined by Thomas Morgan and Captain Cromwell, who had Felicity with him. Introductions were made all around. The small boys edged away from the grownups. There was so much for them to investigate. Tam looked at Felicity, wondering what to say to her. Felicity poked her slippers into clumps of dried seaweed. She eyed Tam's bare feet.

"Don't your feet hurt from the stones and chips of wood?" she asked.

Tam bragged, "My feet are tough. I can walk on anything. I never get slivers in my feet."

Felicity did not know what she could brag about. Finally she said, "I finished my sampler. It has all the letters of the alphabet, a verse from the Bible, and my name and age and the numbers of this year, 1789."

"Pooh," Tam snorted. "I wouldn't learn to do fancywork if I was hung on Gallows Hill for it."

Felicity was shocked. Not so many years ago that was where witches were hung, and some people said the hill was haunted.

Felicity was thoughtful. It was plain to her that Tam did not think she was the precious and talented daughter of the Cromwells that other people thought she was.

Then Tam noticed that the boys had disappeared. Her father and Abigail and the captain were walking around the brig and looking at it from every angle.

"I better find the boys," Tam said. She ran up to higher ground. There was no sign of them. Felicity caught up with Tam and followed her into all the nooks and corners where the boys might have hidden. They had no luck. Felicity said, "I hear voices, but I don't see any boys."

Tam gave her a startled look. "Maybe they fell into the sawing pit," she said.

The girls ran to the pit and peered over the edge. There were Nathaniel and Jamie rolling in the sawdust, laughing and throwing it at each other. Tam looked for the rope ladder that usually hung down one side. But it wasn't there. Jamie began to scream with pain because his eye had sawdust in it.

Tam comforted him: "I'll come down and fix your eye." She leaped into the pit. She worked at Jamie's eye as best she could with a corner of her apron, but he squirmed and yelled and jerked away from her.

Finally she said, "I'll have to take him to Father. He always fixes the carpenters' eyes when they get sawdust in them.

Tam tried to boost Jamie up, but he was too small to reach the edge. "Felicity, you lean over and take his hands and pull him up," Tam ordered.

Felicity bent down, but she couldn't reach the boy.

"Lie on your stomach," Tam said.

With one swift look of dismay at the cluttered ground, Felicity flopped down on her stomach. By leaning far over the pit she managed to reach Jamie's hands. Her hat fell off into the pit. Tam boosted Jamie, and with one hard push he was hauled out of the pit. Nathaniel was next, and then

Tam grabbed Felicity's hands and scrambled out of the pit.

By this time Jamie's howls had brought his father and mother and Captain Cromwell running to see what was going on. Thomas Morgan knelt down, and in a jiffy he had the sawdust out of the boy's eye.

Abigail took one look at the boys. Their hair was thick with sawdust. Tam was surprised that Abigail didn't scold the boys or box their ears the way grownups usually did. She only comforted them and said it was time to go home to get dinner started. The cry of "Grog-ho!" went up in the shipyard, and that meant it was eleven o'clock.

Another surprise for Tam was to hear Felicity tell her father she had had so much fun with Tam and the boys that she wanted to come again to the shipyard.

Captain Cromwell looked at Felicity's rumpled, stained frock and her scratched kid slippers. "Where is your hat?" he asked.

Felicity giggled. "In the pit. I'll jump in and get it." She ran to the pit, followed by Tam, who was yelling, "Don't jump in. Wait until I find the ladder."

But Felicity was feeling something so new and thrilling that she paid no attention to Tam. The others hurried after the girls. Felicity, with one shriek of excitement, leaped into the pit. Tam jumped after her. The girls screamed with high spirits and floundered around in the soft sawdust. Thomas Morgan called one of his carpenters who had finished his morning's grog to bring the rope ladder. He fastened it to the edge. Felicity climbed out, squealing at the unsteadiness of the ladder, and Tam came after her.

"Well—well," Captain Cromwell said with astonishment. "I didn't know you were so nimble, Felicity."

Tam spoke up. "She's nimble. But not as nimble as a rigger, and everybody knows they can climb like monkeys when they rig a ship."

She turned to Felicity. "You must be here when the riggers come. It's lots of fun to see."

Felicity grinned. Her face was dirty and her hair tumbled down over her eyes. The rescued hat had sawdust in its ribbon loops. Captain Cromwell's eyes twinkled. He thought Tam would be a good companion for Felicity. She already looked healthier and happier than he ever remembered.

Then some unexpected matters came up before Abigail and her new family started for home. It was impossible for Captain Cromwell and Thomas Morgan to leave the shipyard for several hours.

The captain said, "Felicity, could you find your way home alone?"

He was worried. Felicity had been so sheltered and protected by her fond mother that she had never had such a long walk alone.

She looked doubtful. "Don't I go along Main Street to School Street and then turn down a lane? Which lane?"

The captain started to give her such detailed directions that she looked more and more doubtful. Thomas Morgan suggested that Felicity go to his house for dinner and that Tam could take her

home afterward. The captain and Thomas Morgan were planning to eat their dinner at the Cat and Wheel. Tam heard Felicity sigh with relief. Her father said to wait until he came later.

"She is scared to walk home alone," Tam thought to herself. Aloud she said, "Come along with us. I'll race you to Derby Street."

Tam dashed headlong, but Felicity was far behind. She didn't run very fast, Tam decided. Finally they arrived at Browne's Lane, and Felicity was wide-eyed when she entered the small house. The low ceilings, the sanded floor, the diamond-paned casement windows were very different from the Cromwells' mansion and those of her relatives. But there was a warm cozy feeling that made her beam with pleasure. The hot dinner that Abigail served from iron pots into pewter plates was delicious. So was the Indian pudding smothered with thick yellow cream.

"You don't eat any more than a bird," Abigail said.

Felicity assured her that she had eaten an enormous meal for her.

After the dishes were washed and put back on the dresser shelves, Abigail said, "Tam, let's have a holiday. I want to see that figurehead Mr. Carter is carving for the brig."

Tam scowled. That meant that if Jeff were home he would see Felicity. And again a sharp bitter pang shook her heart. Jeff had called her a jealous pig. Maybe the pain she felt was jealousy. Dr. Bentley had preached to his congregation that jealousy was a great sin. He said jealousy was selfishness, because one did not want to share. Tam couldn't figure out much of what the good man preached, but she decided to try her best to be sweet and kind to Felicity, even if it did make her angry to see Jeff transfer his admiration from her to Felicity.

They all proceeded down Browne's Lane in the direction of the Carters' house. Watchful neighbors didn't know what to think of a housekeeper without a care in the world strolling with a batch of children. No one could make out who the well-dressed girl was. She certainly did not belong in Browne's Lane.

It happened that Jeff wasn't home when the visitors arrived at the barn studio. When Mr. Carter saw Mistress Morgan, he was pleased and changed his usual cranky expression he wore when interrupted. Felicity charmed him with her fashionable manners, but he warned the small boys not to touch a thing. The figurehead was beginning to look very handsome. "She doesn't look like me,"

Tam exclaimed. "She is a grown-up lady, and what does she hold in her hand?"

"That is a cluster of grapes and apples and leaves. With the other hand she holds back her gown, and her slipper is resting on a scroll that is carved to represent the waves of the ocean. Now when it is all painted you will be able to see exactly what I am showing you."

Felicity spoke up. "I like her hair. It is like Tam's hair, all short curls."

Tam shrieked, "It *is* my hair! And the chin is mine too!" She grabbed Felicity around the waist and whirled her around and around. Tam didn't know how to express her feelings unless she did something violent. However, Felicity, somewhat dizzy and startled, seemed to understand Tam's demonstration.

"Madam," said Mr. Carter, "will you step into the house? My wife will be eager to meet you."

In a few minutes they entered the Carters' back door, and Mrs. Carter was fluttery with surprise. However, she collected herself enough to brew tea and serve it with ginger cakes. The girls and the little boys sat on the long settle jutting out from the hearth. They had mugs of weak tea with plenty of milk in it. Tam and the boys kicked the back of the settle with their heels and gulped down their tea, but Felicity sat up straight and drank her tea in polite sips and nibbled daintily at her ginger cake.

Then Jeff came in. At the sight of Felicity in his kitchen, drinking tea, he got red as a beet and lost his tongue, until the small boys sprang up and pounced on him with gusto.

"Boys," Abigail said, "don't maul Jeff."

"Oh, I don't mind, ma'am," Jeff said. He didn't know who they were.

Tam spoke up. "These are my brothers, Nathaniel and Jamie."

Mrs. Carter said, "Mistress Morgan, Jeff is my youngest. I have Prudence, who isn't home now. She is seventeen."

It was all so surprising to Jeff that he found a chair in the farthest corner and sat restless and ill at ease. Finally, after seeing him squirm long enough, Tam said, "Jeff, show Felicity your new kite."

Jeff grinned and brought his kite into the kitchen. Felicity had never seen one so close. She had seen them in the sky 'way off in the meadows beyond her house.

"Let's see you fly it," Tam urged. "We can go over to the Common."

Abigail heard Tam. "Don't you want to take the boys along? They will soon be old enough to fly kites. They can learn from Jeff just how he does it."

Tam agreed to take the boys along, and with a swoop they were all out of the house, running down Hardy's Lane to the broad Common.

It was a breezy afternoon. Tam took a turn holding the string after Jeff got the kite high in the sky. Felicity watched its tail of knotted rags zigzag this way and that. She asked to hold the string.

"Please, Jeff," she pleaded. It looked so easy to her.

Jeff twisted the string around her finger. "Now play it out and then wind it up when you want to pull in the kite," he said.

Felicity was enchanted to be at one end of the wonderful kite soaring into the heavens. The wind freshened, and the kite tugged like a live thing trying to be released. She played out the string. She was thrilled. She ran over the uneven ground with her eyes on the kite. She stumbled, and a sudden burst of wind tore the end of the string from her hand. The kite zoomed out, out, out, over the ropewalks, over the tan yard, over Shallop Cove, away, away, away into the airy spaces that spread over the sea.

Stunned and shocked, Jeff watched his new kite

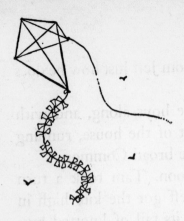

vanish. Tam turned to scold Felicity, but Felicity was sitting in a mud puddle, crying as if her heart would break.

Jeff heard her. He knelt beside her. "Don't cry, Felicity. I can make another kite."

He put his arms around her and lugged her out of the puddle and stood her on her feet. She wept against his shoulder. He was embarrassed. Suppose one of his friends should see him with a girl crying on his shoulder. Tam looked at him with sympathy. She whispered, "Let me hold her." She put strong arms around Felicity and led her to dry ground. The small boys clung to Tam's skirt. They began to cry too. "The kite is gone," Nathaniel wailed. Jamie wept, "The kite is gone, and that horrid girl let it go."

Tam said, "HUSH!" in such a fierce voice that the boys hushed.

Felicity was comforted and assured that no great

tragedy had occurred. They made their way back to the Carters' house. Abigail understood what had happened without much explaining and she soothed Felicity so expertly that soon they were all laughing and teasing Felicity about the state of her frock.

"Come, we'll go home. The captain will soon be there to take Felicity home, and I have our supper to get."

Abigail bustled them to the door. With polite farewells the party trotted off, and Mrs. Carter promised to visit Mistress Morgan very soon.

When Captain Cromwell arrived he was in good humor. Thomas Morgan was a wonderful man. He had handled a difficult situation among some carpenters with tact and understanding. It was a situation that threatened to delay the finishing of the brig.

The captain roared with laughter at the sight of his bedraggled daughter. "Well," he chuckled, "it has been a big day for you."

Then he suggested, after hearing the story about Jeff's lost kite, "You must have your friends visit you one of these days."

Felicity nodded and gave Tam such a happy look that Tam burst out generously, "Jeff will come. I'll bring him."

Tam had seen Dr. Bentley leaving her house and had an uneasy feeling. Her father announced the dreadful news that evening.

"Your mother and Dr. Bentley have decided that you need to go to school. It is high time you went. You'll have to work hard to catch up to the other children of your age. I have made the arrangements and paid down the money. It costs a good deal, but you have to do what you're supposed to do."

Tam could not speak for a few minutes. "But, Father," she stammered, "you—you need me to go to the woods for trunnels."

Thomas Morgan said, "I have all the trunnels I need for this ship."

"But, Father," Tam began again, "you said you didn't believe in school for girls. I can do numbers and write and read well enough."

Her father answered, "Your learning is only that of a small child. You are growing up. Your mother thinks——"

Tam never heard what else her father said. A storm of temper rose furiously, and she gave Abigail a glare of anger and cried, "I hate you!"

Thomas Morgan took Tam by the hand and led her screeching and kicking up the narrow stairs to her attic room. He gave her a spanking and said, "Go to bed. Your mother knows what is best for you." Tam cried herself to sleep.

The next morning Abigail acted as if Tam had never said she hated her. She fixed a big breakfast of mush with milk and honey, fried potatoes, and ham and put up a hearty lunch for Tam to carry to school. "The school bell rings at seven, so you better go along, Tam," she said. "But wait just a minute."

Abigail went to her bedroom and came back with a new tier she had just finished for Tam. It was white and not dark brown. Tam looked at it distrustfully. It was another attempt to make her into a prissy girl. She slipped her arms into it obediently, and Abigail buttoned and tied it in back. She

handed Tam her old straw hat and Tam jammed it on her head. Abigail gave her a loving pat. Tam went out the door looking like a thundercloud.

The school door was open, and the schoolmaster stood there ringing a large hand bell. Tam did not know what to do next. She looked so uncertain that the schoolmaster said, "Well, miss, I suppose you are Tamesine Morgan. I will have to find out where you belong."

In the hubbub that followed, Tam found herself hanging her hat on a peg in a narrow entry and stowing away her lunch. She looked around the big square room. Next to the door there was a fireplace and near it a desk where the schoolmaster sat. He sent the scholars to long backless benches. The benches were in front of a continuous shelf that ran around three sides of the room. There was a smaller shelf underneath for books. The children sat facing the wall, girls on one side and boys on the other.

The morning was spent in examining new scholars to see how much they knew so the schoolmaster could group them accordingly. Tam found herself sitting on the low bench for smaller children. She didn't like that, and she made up her mind to study hard so she would soon be moved to the higher benches for girls of her own age.

At last it was time for lunch. Tam took her bundle handkerchief to the schoolyard and sat under a tree with some girls she knew. They teased Tam because she was in the baby class.

"You just wait," Tam boasted. "I'll go ahead of you all."

There was a frisky tang in the air that made it very hard for the children to go back to the schoolroom at the sound of the bell. The first class was called up to read. Tam saw them step forward to the open space in the middle of the room. They stood in a straight line, toeing the crack in the floor board. Jeff was in the first class, and he had never once given Tam a nod of recognition.

The second class was called on to prepare their pens for writing. The schoolmaster set a copy of a proverb at the top of the page of the copybook. Then he told the newcomers what supplies they had to bring the next day.

Just when Tam thought she couldn't sit still another minute the schoolmaster said, "You may go out." This brief recess was ended when he rapped sharply on the doorpost with a ferrule for them to come in. Each helped himself to a dipper of water from a pail just inside the door.

The second and third classes read from the New Testament, and then Tam's class was called on to read a few easy sentences from the primer. She was pleased to be able to read better than the little ones on her bench, and in the spelling class she could spell louder than any of them.

Finally the bell rang for dismissal. They streamed into the yard, and with one loud screech Tam galloped home as fast as she could. The long day was over at last.

"I'll never get used to sitting in that stuffy schoolroom," Tam told her father at supper. "And I have to have a pen and some ink and a copybook."

Her father nodded. "What class are you in?" he asked.

Tam scowled. "The schoolmaster made me sit with the babies. But I'll leave them soon. Already I am the smartest of them."

Thomas Morgan caught his wife's look of pride in Tam's statement. She said, "You are a very bright girl, Tam. You'll be at the head of your class when you are moved up to sit with girls of your own age."

The days passed. Tam made good her boast and went rapidly into higher classes. But it wasn't any fun. She missed her usual visits to the shipyard and her cronies on the wharves. Then a holiday was announced for a whole week at the end of October because General George Washington was due to visit Salem. Tam felt as if she was going to be let out of a prison. But then the schoolmaster said, "All pupils will meet at ten o'clock on Thursday in Court Street to parade to Buffum's Corner, where we will join the procession."

That was news to Tam. She did not know that all schoolmasters would lead their charges in the parade. She did not like the idea. As soon as the class was dismissed she tagged along with Jeff, and when he parted from his friends she said, "I don't want to be in the parade. We planned to follow it alongside General Washington and that is what we are going to do." They put their heads together and decided to watch at the Mill Dam for General Washington's appearance from Marblehead.

"Why does he visit Marblehead?" Tam asked.

Jeff knew why. "Because in the Revolution the men from Marblehead as well as those from Salem stood by him when times were hard and the victory seemed uncertain."

Tam admired Jeff's high-sounding language and his knowledge of what was going on in the world.

When Thursday came Tam and Jeff were waiting at the Mill Dam. Their families were quite unaware of what they were up to and that they were not going to parade with the school children. They heard cannon shots that signaled General Washington's approach. It was a long wait. At last they saw a large coach drawn by four horses, followed by a baggage wagon with six Negro servants and, most exciting, the white horse the General would ride on later when he reviewed the men in uniform.

"Where is he?" Tam was screaming.

Jeff said, "He is in the coach. Come on!"

They tore alongside the coach, trying to get a look at the man riding inside. They caught a few glimpses of a fine aristocratic profile. Once the General turned and nodded and smiled at the children running along the dusty street.

They galloped until they reached the town pump. The Salem regiment was assembled there, and a regiment from Lynn and the Ipswich Horse in blue.

"We can't get through that crowd," Jeff said. "We'll have to find a good place to watch when they pass."

But all the nearby streets were jammed with different units waiting to enter the parade as soon as General Washington was mounted on his famous white charger.

Jeff said, "If we run around these soldiers we can get to Town House Square before they do, and we can get a good place to hear the General speak."

They knew all the alleys and short cuts, and by dodging in and out they reached the square before it was filled up. The parade went by. Tam and Jeff yelled themselves hoarse cheering the town magistrates, the merchants, mechanics, and, best of all, the shipbuilders.

"Look, there's your father, Jeff—and my father—and there goes our schoolmaster—and listen! Jeff, a band is coming."

The band was playing "Yankee Doodle." Tam thought she would burst, it was all so glorious. But when General Washington was escorted to the balcony by the town officers, she looked straight up at the noble face of the country's hero and she was unable to open her mouth in a cheer. Something of the General's greatness held her spellbound. Then Mr. Goodhue made a grand-sounding speech of welcome, and all Tam remembered of General Washington's answer were his last words, that he hoped their navigation and commerce would flourish and their felicity be complete.

The cheers rang and echoed for a long time, and then the General was taken to Mr. Ward's house for a reception.

By this time everybody was starved. The crowds scattered. Tam said, "Let's go to my house for something to eat, it is the nearest."

When they reached Browne's Lane they found Abigail with two tired, fretful little boys. They had been watching the parade, wanting to see their father much more than the nation's hero. Abigail did not mention the fact that she missed Tam and Jeff in the school children's section.

Tam fixed a big lunch for Jeff and herself. They chattered with Abigail about the important people they had seen in the parade.

Abigail said to Jeff, "Your father looked a very handsome gentleman. What a splendid outfit he wore."

Jeff boasted, "That was his wedding suit. He wore a powdered wig when he was married, but powdered wigs are out of style now. My mother and Prue washed the lace ruffles in the front of his coat and at the cuffs."

Tam said, "I suppose General Washington is in style. He had his hair powdered, and his queue was in a black silk bag. I want to see what he is going to wear this evening. Jeff, we can wait outside Mr. Ward's house and follow him to the Assembly Hall."

Tam looked over the table at Abigail sitting in

her father's big chair with Jamie on her lap. The boy's plump legs stuck out from his skirts, and he sprawled comfortably in her arms, trying to keep awake. At last his eyes stayed shut. Abigail rose and carried him to his bed and laid him beside Nathaniel, who was already asleep.

"Where is Father?" Tam asked.

"Why, didn't you know that Captain Cromwell asked him this morning to go with him to Mr. Ward's house to shake hands with General Washington?" Abigail answered.

Tam was speechless, then she yelled, "Hurrah, hurrah! My father is shaking hands with the General."

She turned to Jeff. "I'm sorry your father isn't having a chance to meet the General."

Jeff looked downcast. But Abigail spoke up. "Why, Jeff, your father was also invited. He is the most celebrated carver hereabouts, and just think how elegant he looks."

Tam was annoyed. She couldn't figure out why people set such a store by handsome clothes. Jeff beamed with delight. "Captain Cromwell is a fine man to work for. I suppose Felicity watched the parade from someone's window."

Tam drew down her brows. Jeff was always wondering what Felicity was doing. She swal-

133

lowed the last crumb of a gingerbread elephant that Abigail loved to bake for her family.

"Let's go, Jeff." Tam was impatient to mingle with the holiday crowds.

Jeff held back. "I ought to go home and see if my mother needs me."

Tam thought that Jeff's mother gave him too many chores. She tempted him, "Let's go past Felicity's house. Maybe she will be outdoors or in the window or something like that, and we could ask her to go with us."

Jeff hesitated only a moment, and then they ran up Browne's Lane toward Felicity's house 'way out on Main Street. The big square mansion with its high ornamental fence in front sat proudly in a green lawn with arching elms and formal flower gardens here and there. Tam and Jeff peered through the palings of the fence. There was no one in sight.

"She isn't home," Tam said. "Let's go downtown."

Jeff was persistent. "Maybe she is in the back garden." He walked to the end of the fence around to the back of the house. High fences surrounded the property's fruit trees and vegetable gardens and stables. Jeff climbed up and managed to look over the top.

Tam scrambled after him, curious about what kept him hanging there. She saw a summerhouse made of latticework. The vines that covered it had lost their leaves and no longer shadowed the interior, for they could see three ladies with heavily fringed Canton shawls draped over their shoulders. They were being served tea by a Negro servant.

Tam could see Felicity shake her head and refuse the tea. She came out of the summerhouse, and she had a tiger-striped kitten in her arms. They watched her break off a long slim branch from a bush and drag it over the grass. She had put the kitten down, and it leaped after the end of the branch. Gradually Felicity drew closer to the fence where Tam and Jeff were clinging by their hands.

Tam rolled her eyes at Jeff. He was grinning from ear to ear.

"Hist!" he whispered.

Felicity looked up, startled to hear the sound.

"Hist!" Jeff repeated.

Felicity's face broke into a smile. She came to the fence. Tam whispered, "Did you see General Washington?"

Felicity said, "Yes, from my uncle's house, but when he went past there were so many people around him that I hardly know what he looks like."

Jeff and Tam exchanged looks. They felt sorry for Felicity. She had missed so much. Tam said, "Come with us. We are going to hang around Mr. Ward's house and follow General Washington to the Assembly Hall. We saw him plain, and you will too if you can come with us."

Felicity was on the edge of tears. She told them her mother would not give her permission to run around the town. In fact, her mother was right now about to go to her room to rest before she dressed for the Assembly Hall, where the men and women of society would honor the General.

Tam whispered, "When your mother goes to her room, you sneak out and meet us at the back gate."

Felicity looked doubtful until Jeff urged her, "You'll surely get to see General Washington close to. I wish you would come."

That made up her mind. "Wait for me. Don't go until I come," she whispered.

They saw her go to the house with the three ladies. They dropped down from the fence and sauntered to the Cromwells' back gate.

Tam and Jeff waited and waited for Felicity. It was after six before she came. She whispered, "I had to pretend I was going to bed before my mother left. The carriage just drove off."

Felicity was excited, and her heart was beating madly.

Tam said, "It is too late to go to Mr. Ward's house because the General is going to be at the Assembly Hall by seven o'clock. We'll go there. Hurry."

When they reached the Hall, a great crowd had gathered to see the General arrive with Mr. Ward. The Hall was already filled with ladies and gentlemen wearing their finest garments. The children prodded, pushed, and elbowed their way until they stood in the front line of spectators.

A loud cheer rang out. "He is coming!" Tam shrieked.

They were sure of seeing the General until a line of the militia made the crowd move back. Felicity was jammed behind a burly back, and she saw nothing of General Washington. The church bells began to ring, and fire rockets went up from the courthouse.

Felicity wept, "I didn't see him at all."

Jeff and Tam tried to comfort her. Jeff had an idea then. "We'll go to the side and climb up to peek in the windows."

Felicity sobbed, "I can't climb."

Jeff said nothing. He darted ahead to investigate. Soon he came back and whispered, "Come with me."

The girls followed him. They stood under a row of windows.

"I climbed up and I could see into the Hall. Felicity, I'll boost you up," Jeff said.

"I'm afraid," Felicity whimpered.

Tam snorted, "Don't be such a fraid cat. I'll help Jeff. We won't let you fall."

Felicity found herself being pushed and boosted up a wall whether she was scared or not, and she scrambled and clutched the sill. She found the window open. She looked in, and there was a blaze of light from hundreds of candles in sconces along the walls and in the crystal chandeliers. The smell of tallow candles wafted out the window to her. She stared into the crowd of people. She saw Dr. Bentley in a fine snuff-colored suit chatting with some ladies. All the ladies seemed to be wearing Washington sashes of black velvet with clasps of gold or silver eagles, and the initials G and W were on either side. As she watched, General Washington, dressed in black velvet, rose from an armchair at the end of the Hall. Dancing began, and she lost sight of him. Then two men came to the window for a breath of fresh air. They were talking together. The one dressed in black velvet turned to the open window. He met the earnest stare of a little girl whose hat had fallen off and hung down her back.

Felicity clung with all her strength to the sill. She could feel Jeff and Tam sagging under her weight. She wanted to speak, but she could not open her mouth. The first President of the country smiled at her. Then her props began to give way and she was lowered to the ground with a swift jar.

Felicity had her breath jolted out of her, and when she could speak she gasped, "I saw General Washington plain! He—he smiled at me!"

Tam hugged her hard. "I'm so glad. Now let's go watch the rockets."

Felicity was wild with the thrilling events of the evening, and she had no desire to go home. General Washington was to leave the party to go to bed at nine o'clock, and she knew that her parents would stay for the dancing the rest of the evening.

The town was crowded with visitors from far and near. They jostled the children and told them to go home to bed. Tam was saucy and answered them impudently. Felicity was too timid to make pert remarks, but she giggled and admired Tam's boldness. Jeff said he was hungry and maybe they ought to take Felicity home.

"You must get home before your father and mother discover that you played truant," he insisted.

Felicity began to droop. It was long past her bedtime, and she was ready to go home. They left her at the back gate.

"I hope nobody catches you coming in," Jeff said. Tam added, "You'll be spanked if you are caught, so be very quiet."

Felicity's weary face broke into a smile. "I have never been spanked." She slipped inside the gate, whispering, "Good night."

"Heavens to Betsy," Tam cried. "You have never been spanked?"

Jeff took a last glimpse of Felicity's face, pale in the dusky evening. "Maybe she will be spanked," he muttered.

They made their way home, planning to meet the next morning to see General Washington ride on his famous white charger to inspect the new North Bridge. From there he would go to Ipswich on his way back to Boston.

When Tam got home she found her father waiting up for her. "I thought you would never come home, lass," he said. "It is long after ten o'clock."

"I know, Father, but——" Tam yawned. "It was such fun to see the rockets go up into the sky——" She yawned again.

"I'm hungry," she managed to say between yawns.

Her father set out a mug of milk and some rye and Injun bread plastered with butter. Tam drank the milk and chewed diligently on the bread. Then her head fell forward. With eyes already closed she pillowed her head on her arms and was fast asleep.

Thomas Morgan picked her up and carried her to bed. He helped her to undress. She seemed unconscious of everything and never remembered the next morning how he had tended her as if she were a baby.

Friday was full of adventure for Tam and Jeff. They saw the General ride over the flag-bedecked bridge. After that they roamed the woods for black walnuts and butternuts. Saturday Jeff went off with some boys to go fishing. Tam had to go to a sail loft for Abigail.

"Get a bunch of thrums for me, Tam. And do take Nathaniel with you. He is teasing Jamie and making him cry."

At first Tam had thought it fun to have two small brothers, but lately she had begun to think that having a small boy or two tagging after was a drag on her usual galloping here and there.

But Nathaniel was eager to go with Tam, and they set off for the nearest sail loft. Up the stairs they climbed to the great room with its polished floor, where men sat cross-legged. Around them were spread the immense white sheets of new canvas. It was a quiet room lit by small-paned dusty windows.

One of the men who knew what the appearance of a child meant got up from the floor and said, "You want a bunch of thrums, Tam?"

She nodded. There was something about the huge dusty sail loft with its smell of newly woven canvas and of tar that gave wings to her imagination. These sheets of canvas were to billow out with

143

the wind and send Salem's ships on their voyages to foreign lands and to bring them home with their romantic cargoes.

Nathaniel, however, had his eyes fixed on the sailmaker's hand.

"What's that?" he asked.

The sailmaker told Nathaniel it was a thimble. It was fastened in the middle of his palm.

Tam stared out a narrow window. She could see the life of Salem's water front going on below her. She loved the bustle and stir of unloading cargoes, of sailors rolling down the wharves, of the merchants running back and forth from the cargoes to their countinghouses. She could see Captain Cromwell's brig growing more and more solid-looking. She heard the sound of ax blows, the screech of the saw, and the creak of tackle. From farther off came the clang of white-hot iron being pounded on the blacksmith's anvil into a cross-brace strap.

"Here you are, Tam." She turned from the window and took the short pieces of rope yarn that people used for tying up bundles. She thanked the sailmaker and hauled Nathaniel, bellowing with rage, down the rickety steps.

"I wanted to stay there," Nathaniel howled. "I was sliding on the floor, and it was like sliding on slippery ice."

Tam said, "We'll go look at Father's ship if you stop crying."

Nathaniel stopped at once and trotted along with Tam to the shipyard. He yelled with delight at seeing his father. Thomas Morgan was proud of his son and showed him off to his carpenters. Tam, however, wondered just what her father's strange glance at her meant.

"I wonder what I have done now that I shouldn't have done," she said to herself. She soon found out, for Captain Cromwell came from around a corner, and when he saw her he stopped and eyed her with that same look. A light dawned on her. Probably Felicity had been caught last Thursday night and had told her father that Tam and Jeff were to blame for her naughtiness. Tam bobbed politely to the captain.

Captain Cromwell said, "I suppose you saw the President outside the Assembly Hall?"

"Who?" Tam asked.

"I mean General George Washington," he answered.

Tam answered honestly, "No, I didn't see him because I was behind a row of soldiers."

"Humph," the captain grunted. "That's too bad."

Tam spoke up. "I did see him in the parade and

in his carriage and the next morning at North Bridge."

"Felicity saw him plain, she told me. Now I wonder how that came about? I wonder . . ." The captain's voice was peculiar, Tam thought. It sounded as if he really wasn't angry. It sounded almost as if he was trying not to laugh. She wondered how much Felicity had told of her adventure, for her father didn't seem to know all that had happened.

The bells rang for dinnertime, and everybody scurried off to eat a hot meal or to open their lunch pails. Captain Cromwell went off. Thomas Morgan urged his children to hurry along. On the way home he said, "Captain Cromwell told me that Felicity was discovered coming into the house very late Thursday night by a servant girl. Felicity confessed that she had been to see General Washington, and she refused to tell who she was with. Because the girl had always been obedient and not accustomed to roaming the streets alone, her father thinks she must have been with some other children."

Tam asked, "Did she get spanked?"

"Now how would I know that?" Her father was surprised at the question. "Did you have anything to do with the matter?"

146

Tam did not know how to answer the question without getting Felicity into more trouble, so she asked a question instead.

"How did they know where she went?"

Thomas Morgan said, "Felicity managed to climb up to look into an open window. A friend of her father's was chatting with the General, and he was the one who recognized her. Before he could get a look at who was helping her, she dropped down and disappeared. He could see that the window was so high up from the ground that someone had been holding her."

"My," Tam murmured, "I would never think that sissy could do such a thing."

"No," her father agreed. "It sounds more like something you would do."

Tam was thankful that her father did not force her any further. She didn't know what would be the right thing to do—to confess her part in the adventure or to let Felicity keep her secret and remain loyal to Tam and Jeff.

She said to herself, "Felicity isn't a telltale, and I guess she isn't a sissy all the time." Then she felt a prick of envy. "She is going to christen the brig, and Jeff will think she is more wonderful than ever."

School kept Tam so busy that she didn't get into much mischief, and the neighbors said to each other that perhaps Tam would turn out to be a ladylike girl after all. She did not whistle or yell the way she did a short while ago. But this state of affairs came to a quick close one day in January. It was a day when the boys and girls carried their skates to school so they could go directly from school to one of the favorite ponds.

All Tam owned was a pair of trunks that children learned on. The clumsy pieces of wood about an inch square, turning up at the heel, with straps to fasten over the foot, were getting too short for Tam's growing feet. But she had nothing else to skate on.

Tam hung around in the school entry looking at the skates. Some were made of iron, and there was a pair of Holland skates and several curve skates. The schoolmaster was very cranky that morning because he had a stuffy head cold to add to his usual ill humor. He glared at Tam, who was in an impudent, mischievous mood that morning. She had a way of making the girls on her bench act restless, and she started them whispering and giggling. When they stood up to toe the crack and recite their lessons, the schoolmaster was stricter than usual. He couldn't scold Tam for not knowing her lessons because she was always at the head of her class.

The schoolmaster's frown made Tam rebellious. She knew he was going to make her copy over some dull proverb when the time came. He was going to find fault with her quill pen—it wouldn't be properly sharpened, or else her curlicues in making capital letters would bring his ferrule down sharply on her fingers.

School was impossible, she decided. When he let

the scholars out for a few minutes in the middle of the morning, she lingered in the entry, and when no one was looking she grabbed the pair of shining Holland skates and disappeared.

Tam had a wonderful time with the keen-bladed skates. The January day was sunny and cold. Her nose grew red and her cheeks flamed. The quilted hood she wore fell back on her head, and her curls gleamed red in the sunlight. The ringing sound of the skates on the ice was music. "Oh, I wish I had skates like these," she said to herself.

In the distance the bells rang out for noon. "I'm hungry," she said. The skates screeched to a stop in a shower of powdered ice. She didn't know whose skates she had on, but she hoped to get them back before the owner discovered they were gone. She ran back to the school. The children were going in. They had already eaten their dinners.

The schoolmaster was ringing the bell. Tam held the skates behind her back. But it was no use. A cry went up from one of the older girls. "Tam Morgan has my skates. She stole them."

"I did not steal them," Tam declared. "I only borrowed them."

She pushed into the entry to get her dinner. She was starved. But the schoolmaster laid a hand on her shoulder.

"I am going to punish you, miss. You will not eat your dinner." He forced her to his desk and picked up his rod and whipped her. Tam did not make a sound. Whipping went on nearly every day, and it was a point in pride not to whimper. But Tam's punishment was not over. The schoolmaster went out and cut a branch from a tree. He made a split in the large end of it. To Tam's embarrassment, he sprung that end on her nose.

"Now, miss, you stand here and let the others see what happens to disobedient girls who run away from classes."

A snicker went up. Tam looked very funny standing with the spreading branch of dried leaves pinching her nose like a clothespin. She had to breathe through her mouth, and it grew dry. She was thirsty and so hungry that her stomach made little complaining noises. She scowled at the small children nudging each other and kicking each other's shins. They were delighted to have something more entertaining than trying to learn to read and write.

Tam shifted from one foot to the other. She didn't know how much longer she could stand the pinching on her nose. She felt a smarting in her eyes and she grew frantic. Not for anything did she

152

want to cry. That was exactly what the school-master was waiting for.

Tam rolled her eyes to the side of the room where the boys were doing their copy work. Jeff lifted his head to give her a swift warm grin of complete admiration. Tam felt better at once. Jeff still thought she was a brave girl. He had not given all his affection to Felicity. She kept thinking about her and remembering that Captain Cromwell said Felicity was to have a party and invite Tam and Jeff. It was a long time since she had seen the captain, and perhaps after Felicity's adventure in October he thought that Tam and Jeff were not proper friends for his daughter. Of course Tam was only guessing that the captain knew what part they had played in her adventure. Tam was so busy keeping her mind on Felicity and the amazing fact that a girl was going to christen the brig that the pinching branch did not bother her so much. Her nose didn't seem to have any more feeling in it.

The lessons went on. The spelling classes shouted together. The readers stumbled over long words. Then it was time to let the pupils out in the yard for a few minutes.

The schoolmaster came to take the branch from Tam's nose. She put her hand up, and there was no feeling at the end of her nose. She ran out with the others. They said she looked queer because the end of her nose was white. Soon it began to throb and burn, and when Tam reached home with her dinner still uneaten it was swollen and red.

Abigail was shocked to hear what had happened to Tam's nose. "That is dreadful. Of course schoolmasters have to whip children, but who ever thought of such a cruel punishment? And of course you shouldn't have taken the skates and run away from school."

She made cloth packs and soaked them in cold water. Tam held them on her nose until it began to feel better. Abigail had a good supper of a roast and vegetable, a cranberry pie and a squash pie and rice pudding. Tam's appetite was enormous.

Abigail told Thomas Morgan that Tam's trunks were too short for her and that she was old enough to own a pair of Holland skates. Thomas Morgan approved Abigail's suggestions and ideas. She seemed to know what was proper for Tam, and besides, Tam had turned out to be such a good scholar that he was growing proud of her learning, in spite of the fact that he used to think girls didn't need an education.

"I'll get your skates tomorrow," he said.

But Tam did not get her skates the next day because Thomas Morgan was sick. He had a fever, and Abigail prepared drinks of cooling tamarind water. But it did no good. After three days she sent Tam for the doctor. He came and found Thomas Morgan so sick that he decided to sit by his bed and watch him through the night.

Tam thought he was an impressive-looking man in his claret-colored suit with buttons of silver coins. The full-skirted coat had huge pockets, and so did his waistcoat. The doctor laid his cocked hat on a table in the kitchen. He was wearing his every-day wig made of horsehair, and his queue was tucked into a stiff bag made of eel skin.

Abigail was worried. Thomas Morgan didn't know her. He tossed and moaned and begged for water, which the doctor claimed was bad for him. Abigail and Tam sat watching the sick man. They dozed finally in their chairs, worn out with watching. The doctor nodded too.

A candle on the table at his elbow burned brightly. The doctor's head jerked. He was trying to stay awake. Instantly there was a sharp explosion, a hissing sizzle, and much smoke. Abigail and Tam dropped to the floor and scrambled under the valance of the bed for safety.

The doctor fumbled for his wig, but his shaven head was scorched and bare. He was not fully awake. But Thomas Morgan was awakened by the explosion. He jumped from his bed and poured a pitcher of water on the doctor's head. Then he flopped back into his bed and laughed and laughed at the comical appearance of the doctor.

Tam and Abigail crept out from under the bed. They stared at the sick man and then at the doctor. They began to laugh too. Abigail's laughter changed to tears, for she saw that her husband was no longer delirious but looking as if he was going to get well very quickly.

Tam picked up the doctor's wig, smelling vilely of burned horsehair and eelskin. It was still smoldering.

"Throw it in the fire, my girl," said the doctor.

She held it out at arm's length and ran to the fireplace and threw it far back into the roaring fire.

The doctor pulled out his big handkerchief and tied it over his bare head. He had no wig to keep it warm.

"I'm sorry about your wig and the eelskin bag that exploded from the candle," Abigail ventured.

"Ho," he laughed. "I have a better wig for Sundays. I may as well wear it out. They say wigs are going out of style. It was worth it to see your husband make such a remarkable recovery."

Abigail paid the doctor, and he bowed himself out and pulled his cocked hat well over the handkerchief. They heard the hoof clops of his horse fade away down the lane.

The next day Thomas Morgan sat at the fireplace, growing stronger by the minute. In three days he was back at work, and when he came home one day he had a pair of gleaming skates for Tam. She laughed with joy to see them.

Her father told her, "Captain Cromwell was buying skates for Felicity. He thinks she ought to learn to skate and he has hired an instructor for her."

"Does somebody have to teach her how to skate?" Tam was surprised.

"Of course. It is just the same as having a dancing teacher or a riding teacher," her father explained.

Tam boasted, "I can do all those things without having a teacher. We learn from each other." She added, "I wish I could see Felicity skate."

"That reminds me," her father said, "Captain Cromwell has seen the figurehead. It is painted and ready for the day when the brig is further along."

"Oh Father, when will the brig be launched?" Tam cried.

"I expect in May, but what she is to be named is still a secret. I'm not sure whether or not Captain Cromwell himself knows."

158

Tam looked pensive. "I knew that name. I spoke it in a dream, and then you woke me up too soon and I can't remember what it was."

Her father smiled, as if her dreams were of no importance, but Tam decided that she must try hard to have that dream again.

Tam woke one morning in February and poked her head out from under the covers. It was so cold that she didn't want to leave her warm nest. She heard her father call up the stairway, "Tam, lass coom down and dress by the fire."

Tam made a dash for the washstand. She broke the ice in her blue-and-white pitcher and poured water in the bowl. The shock of cold water on her face woke her up thoroughly. She dried herself vigorously and took off her nightcap.

Then she put her mouth close to the frosted windowpane and breathed on it until there was a clear space to look out. She scratched with her fingernails to make it larger and then peered out.

There was deep snow on everything. The rising

sun made a ship, sheathed in ice, glitter as if it were made of crystal. A fisherman was breaking through the harbor's ice to make a long channel of open water. Tam blinked in the glare of the sun on the ice. Then clutching her clothes, she flew down to the hearth.

Abigail was frying potatoes and chops. The little boys were tumbling together like puppies. It was cheerful. Tam remembered how hard it had been last winter for her to fix a hearty meal for her father and herself while he shoveled out paths and brought in buckets of water and more firewood. No one could say that he looked pookit this winter.

"Tam," Abigail said when breakfast was over, "stop at Debbie Saltmarsh's for some needles and thread when school is over, and here is a penny for candy."

Tam's brows drew down in a scowl. She had planned to go sliding with some girls after school. There was a steep hill in back of the schoolhouse, and they were taking their sleds to school with them.

But Tam was changing a little. She was learning to think of others. Abigail was so good to Tam and she never forgot to keep promises to Tam, who had seldom kept promises.

It was hard to leave the gay youngsters pulling

their sleds to the hill, and Tam was tempted to stay and have fun, but she trudged dutifully down Main Street and did the errand and bought a blackjack. She thrust the chubby stick in her mouth. It tasted of molasses, butter, and brown sugar, with a faint trace of maple syrup, so sweet and delicious that nothing could be compared to it.

Main Street was lively with sleighs drawn by horses with jingling bells on their harnesses. Tam stood watching the traffic. Some heavy horses plodded along pulling pungs, and then she saw Captain Cromwell in his brightly painted sleigh. He had a black bearskin robe over his lap. Mrs. Cromwell sat beside him, and only the tip of her nose was visible from under the deep quilted bonnet she wore.

Tam longed with all her heart to drive in that beautiful sleigh between the snowbanks. The prancing black horses, their bells all in tune, made a glorious jingle. Felicity probably drove in that sleigh and cuddled into that bearskin robe. Tam was interrupted by a croaking voice: "Where did ye get that blackjack?"

She turned to see Peg-leg Jeggles hopping along on his wooden pin.

"Hey," she called, "wait for me."

Peg-leg waited, and together they made their

way through the crowds of busy people bustling up and down Main Street.

"Don't see much of ye since school took ye off the wharves," Peg-leg said. "Are ye smart?"

Tam laughed. "Smart enough, but I'll be glad when school is over. I don't get to see the brig very often, and Jeff's father is putting on the scroll-work, and I haven't seen the figurehead, either, for a long time."

"Heh," Peg-leg chuckled. "Wait here, I got to go in and get a plug of tobaccy."

Tam stopped at the wooden Indian and brushed off the high white turban of snow that topped his feathered headdress. She scooped the snow off his bunch of tobacco leaves. She was so busy cleaning off snow that she did not hear herself being spoken to for a moment.

She turned to the voice and quickly dropped a curtsy the way Abigail had been teaching her. It was Dr. Bentley, Salem's well-known preacher.

He was surprised to see Tam act politely, and to himself he said that the new Mistress Morgan was doing a fine job in training that motherless, wild Tamesine Morgan.

"Tamesine," he said, "do you like to sing?"

Tam said, "No." She added, "Sir."

"Oh." Dr. Bentley was disappointed. "I am

looking for new members for the Singing Society." Tam had enough learning going to school. She said positively, "No, sir."

She was not going to get tied up with any of his schemes. She knew that he was to blame for her having to go to school.

"Well—well." The good man wasn't used to such frankness and he did not know how to proceed with his hopes to get Tam under his wing and help train her to be a well-behaved young girl.

He was saved by the appearance of Peg-leg Jeggles, who bobbed his head and pulled his forelock in respect to Dr. Bentley. He watched the pair go amiably along the street chattering like old cronies.

Tam had to hear all the news of ships and where they had last been spoken and on what seas, and who had been lost at sea. She had to hear the romantic stories some sailors told of Chinese ladies with tiny bound feet and men wearing embroidered robes like skirts and boasting of their long finger-nails.

Tam was again in the enchanted world of the water front. She could hardly bear to leave Peg-leg and his stories. She begged him to come home with her for supper. Peg-leg was bashful. "What would your father say to have an old wharf rat like me sit at his table?"

Tam's pleas were hard to resist. The thought of a meal in a cozy small house with a handsome young woman bending over the pots hanging in the fireplace and serving hot food to famished menfolk was too attractive to pass by.

When Tam came in, followed by the thump of a wooden leg, the small boys ran to see who it was. Tam cried out, "I brought Peg-leg Jeggles to have supper with us."

Abigail quickly recovered from her astonishment and greeted him warmly. When Thomas Morgan came in with the buckets of water, he saw Peg-leg being pushed into a chair, with the two boys clinging to his wooden leg, trying to find out how it was fastened on.

Peg-leg Jeggles was treated like an honored guest, and the evening promised to be exciting as soon as he was filled up with food. Just when the family had eaten supper and was ready to be entertained there was a knock at the door.

Thomas Morgan opened it. He saw Captain Cromwell's colored manservant. At first Thomas Morgan was frightened, thinking some accident or disaster had happened to the captain, but the man grinned and held out a note. "For Mistress Tamesine Morgan," he said, and bowed and left.

Tam sprang up, crying, "For me! I never had a note in all my life!"

She unfolded the paper, and her eyes flew over the words. "I'm invited to a party! February twenty-seventh from five to ten o'clock." She squealed between each phrase and jumped up and down.

"I wonder if Jeff got his invitation this evening. I can't wait to ask him." She spun around like a top, and Peg-leg shook with laughter until his rosy cheeks looked more and more like wrinkled winter apples. The little boys climbed all over him, and even if he didn't get to tell many stories because of the excitement brought about by Felicity's invitation, they all had a fine evening until the boys were so wild they had to be sent to bed.

When Peg-leg hopped out into the snowy lane, he carried a bundle of ginger cake, corn bread, and cheese tied up with thrums.

The next day being Saturday, Tam could hardly wait to see Jeff. After helping Abigail with Saturday's extra cooking and cleaning, she put on her quilted hood and bottle-green cloak.

"Tam," Abigail said, "take the boys with you on the sled. I don't want them underfoot because I want to put my mind on something with no interruptions."

Tam agreed without a murmur of protest. It was slower going with the sled, and the boys were heavily bundled in their coats and mufflers. Nathaniel's legs were growing long, and it was hard for him to keep his feet up on the sled.

"When I am seven," he said, "I'll wear breeches and be a big boy, but Jamie will have to keep on wearing skirts for a long time."

Jamie's ears were completely deafened with layers of wool tied over his head, or a squabble would have begun. Tam hauled the sled into the Carters' yard. The boys were already jumping into the snowbanks along each neatly carved-out path when Mrs. Carter, hearing their yelps of delight, came to the door. It bothered her to see the immaculate stretches of snow filled with hollows.

"Come in, children, keep out of the snow," she called. Her teeth chattered with the icy wind blowing over the harbor. "Hurry up!" she managed to say.

Tam, mindful of Mrs. Carter's crazy ideas of neatness, brushed off the boys before they went into the big kitchen. The boys made a dash for the two cats sleeping in Mr. Carter's rocking chair. They squeezed them so lovingly that the cats yowled and leaped from their arms. Tam asked for Jeff.

"He is out with his father, sweeping up chips in the workroom."

Before Mrs. Carter could say another word, Tam was outdoors, across the yard, and into the big chilly workroom that Mr. Carter called his studio.

"Jeff," she cried, "I got an invitation from Felicity to a party, did you?"

Jeff's face was all smiles. "Yes, last night Captain Cromwell's manservant brought me an invitation. I'll answer it today."

"Oh"—Tam was surprised—"do we have to write a note to say we are coming?"

Mr. Carter broke in, "Of course. That is proper manners. And the note must be sent by hand."

"What do you mean, by hand?" Tam asked.

Mr. Carter explained that a servant should present the note at the door. Tam didn't think that they had any letter paper at home, but Jeff said Prudence had some and was giving him a sheet and perhaps she would give one to Tam. Mr. Carter told the children to run along, but Tam suddenly remembered the figurehead, and she ran back to look at it.

"My," she gasped, "isn't it beautiful? The colors are so bright, and she doesn't look as stuck up as other figureheads do with their noses in the air.

Why, she has a happy look, as if she loved breasting the waves and going to foreign seas." Tam was spellbound.

Mr. Carter was pleased to hear Tam's words about the figurehead. "Ah yes," he sighed half to himself, "she is a felicitous creature."

Tam didn't know what "felicitous" meant and she was too eager to get at the writing of her acceptance to linger and ask him.

Prue was generous with her letter paper, and soon Tam and Jeff sat at the table with freshly sharpened quill pens and a bottle of fine ink to write their notes. Prue told them what to write. Then came the question as to who they could send with the notes. Neither had money to pay for a hired messenger. Tam was thoughtful, and then she said, "We can send Nathaniel. We will haul the boys on the sled up to Captain Cromwell's front gate and send Nathaniel to the door."

Jeff thought it a good idea. The boys were glad to have another ride, and they set off into the snowy lanes. It was a long trip, and there were many interruptions as they took a look into a shop-window or threw snowballs at school friends or just stopped and discussed the party and what it would be like. Neither had ever been to such a fashionable party before.

When they reached the Cromwells' gate, Nathaniel became stubborn and refused to go to the front door. Tam promised him everything she could think of, but Nathaniel was not to be persuaded. But then Jeff said, "You're a big boy, too big to be wearing skirts, and you are not scared to rap on the door and hand the notes to a servant, are you?"

Nathaniel stood up, making himself as tall as possible, and he struck out with a stride that made Tam giggle. "He is walking just like Father," she told Jeff.

They watched through the palings of the fence. The door opened, and a maid wearing an enormous mobcap stood there. She was about to slam the door, thinking Nathaniel was some bold urchin, when she saw the notes he held out. Nathaniel announced in a little-boy squeak, "For Mistress Felicity——" He forgot the rest of the name and turned and ran back to Tam, yelling, "I forgot the rest of the name."

The maid stood in the doorway, bewildered, until Nathaniel returned, shouting, "Cromwell."

She laughed then and thanked him and shut the door.

Jeff continued to peer through the fence, hoping to have a glimpse of Felicity. "Come, Jeff,"

CHAPTER 12

Tam urged. "Let's go sliding on schoolhouse hill."

Jeff turned away. Not a curtain stirred. Felicity had not come to the window to see who had brought the notes. He was disappointed and wanted to stay near the mansion, but Tam and the boys yelled at him until he took the rope with Tam and started running, with the boys hanging on for dear life.

It was too late to slide on the schoolhouse hill, for the bells were pealing and the boys were hungry and cold. Tam and Jeff made plans to skate in the afternoon. They called good-by to each other when Tam turned to go toward Browne's Lane with the complaining boys. She felt a little grumpy. She thought of the beautiful figurehead for the brig that Felicity was going to christen. She wished she could be Felicity for just that one time.

As the day of the party drew near, Tam began to wonder if all the fuss Abigail was making over what Tam should wear was worth the party. Abigail had forbidden Tam to chop off her curls quite a while back, and now her curls were beginning to cluster on her neck and to need a ribbon to keep them from falling over her eyes.

"It is silly to wear ribbons," Tam complained. But Abigail managed to have her way with Tam somehow, without Tam knowing exactly how it came about.

Abigail had been sewing ever since the invitation came, and she had made a fashionable black silk apron with a bib. Tam also had a new woolen dress. It was a shade of brown like pale amber, and it brought out the golden glints in her eyes and made her curls take on a golden sheen when they were brushed diligently. Tam had to brush and comb her curls everyday and she had to scrub hard at her ears and neck. The freckles Jeff teased her about had faded some during the winter, but they still gave her skin a healthy tan.

At last it was time to go to the party. Jeff came along looking so clean and polished that Tam laughed. It was a nervous laugh and petered out quickly. Tam felt queer. She had never been scared about anything before and she did not like the feeling. Jeff, however, was beaming. He urged Tam to walk faster. She said her shoes pinched. Somehow she wasn't as eager to reach the captain's mansion as Jeff was, who thought only of seeing Felicity and being with her for a few hours.

Neither Tam nor Jeff had given a thought to other guests, and they lost their tongues when the maidservant with the big mobcap showed them upstairs to the large square bedrooms where they would take off their wraps.

Three girls were in the room when Tam entered. They were primping before a full-length French mirror. Tam stared into the mirror. She looked so different. The girls wore silk dresses that rustled when they moved. They examined each other's jewelry. One girl wore little soft ostrich feathers in her hair. Tam's eyes dropped to their slippers. They were of pale-colored silk, and she could see her own stout leather shoes made by a cobbler in Browne's Lane.

The girls twittered like sparrows in the eaves, Tam thought. After their first greetings they had nothing more to say to Tam. When they started to go down the broad stairs, Tam went slowly, looking at the marble statues in the niches and the paintings on the walls. She followed the girls into a large room at one side of the entrance hall. Felicity came forward to greet her guests. Each curtsied and made polite remarks.

Tam's heart was jumping around inside, and for the first time in her life she wished she were pretty and dainty and fashionable like Felicity. She thought Felicity looked just like the fashion dolls from Paris that were displayed in the shopwindows to show the Salem ladies the latest styles.

Tam stuck her hands in her apron pockets and stood with feet planted solidly apart. Her eyes were wistful. She felt she didn't belong in the mansion. Jeff was standing with the boys on one side of the room. He was not dressed in a velvet suit like the other boys, but he appeared perfectly at home.

When Felicity said they were going to dance the minuet, Jeff darted forward and asked her to be his

partner. A young woman Felicity called Aunt Jane played the spinet.

A lanky boy who had no partner shuffled over to Tam and asked her to be his partner. She hated him at once.

"Pooh," she snorted, "I don't want to dance that silly minuet."

She did not know how to dance the minuet, but she would not admit it. The boy was shocked. The girls he knew didn't talk so bold. He was too embarrassed to do anything but stand on one foot and then the other and to fumble with a tassel holding back the window draperies. He wished himself miles away from the rude girl.

The minuet was over. Somebody wanted to play the Needle's Eye. A circle was formed, and Tam found herself urged into it by Aunt Jane. A boy and a girl made a bridge, and the circle marched under it, singing:

> "Needle's eye that doth supply
> The thread that runs so true:
> Many a beau have I let go,
> Because I wanted you."

When the word "you" was reached, the arms came down on a captive, who was taken aside and asked, "Do you like figs or dates better?"

Tam said, "Dates."

She was told to stand behind the girl called Sally. When all the children had been caught they had a tug of war. Tam clasped her strong arms around Sally and pulled with such vigor that her side won. But Tam had yanked so hard that she tore Sally's delicate frock, and that made Sally burst into tears.

Aunt Jane took Sally upstairs to repair the damage as best she could. She suggested that they play a quiet game. Some played chess and others cards. Jeff persuaded Felicity to play on the spinet. Tam stood by watching Jeff's face. Felicity smiled up at him, and she smiled as sweetly at Tam. She finished the piece and drew them to a corner of the room to whisper about the time they had seen General Washington.

"Did you get spanked?" Tam asked.

"Yes," Felicity giggled. "But it didn't hurt."

"Did you cry?" Jeff asked.

Felicity said, "Of course not, and I did not tell them how I got to see General Washington at the open window."

Tam's heart grew warmer. "I think you are a—a—a chip off the old block." That was the highest praise she could give.

They were interrupted by Mrs. Cromwell inviting them into the dining room. From then on everyone ate nuts and raisins, hot biscuits, pound cakes and sponge cakes, desserts in fancy shapes, and custards. They drank tea or coffee and hot and cold punch.

Tam ate heartily. She was always hungry. Mrs. Cromwell saw that everybody was busy eating and that her servants kept the table well supplied with more and more food. She knew all the children except Tam and Jeff. Felicity had made the proper introductions, and Tam and Jeff had made their manners.

Mrs. Cromwell's eyes went over Tam's outfit, and Tam was pleased to have her say, "You look charming, my dear. I have heard about you from Felicity's father."

Tam wondered just what she had heard and if she had any suspicion of the part Tam had played in Felicity's adventure.

The children went back to the parlor and chattered about the parade for General George Washington. Tam spoke up: "I saw the General plain, so did Jeff."

One of the boys said, "Why do you call him General? He is President Washington."

"He is not," Tam cried out. "He is General George Washington."

"You goose," the boy jeered. "Don't you know anything?"

"I know more than you do," Tam snapped back. She marched close to the boy. "I can lick you any day." She put up her fists. A flash of temper took her unaware, and before she knew it she had punched the boy on the nose. To her dismay, the nose began to bleed. Gasps of horror went up from the boys and cries of "Shame on you to strike Henry" from the girls.

Tam was mortified. All she wanted to do was to get away from the cries of reproach. She slipped into the hall and blindly opened the outside door. Then she knew she should not run away. She slammed the door shut and opened another door into a second parlor. A gust of wind blew in from the opening and shutting of doors.

Tam stood still. The beautiful room had a tranquillity that soothed her troubled heart. "I guess I'm a naughty girl," she admitted.

Then she saw two Chinese figures in the corners of the room. Their heads began to nod. They agreed that she was a naughty girl. Tam's mouth opened in complete surprise.

The figures were of a man and a woman about four feet high, dressed in embroidered coats and embroidered shoes. The lady had an elaborate headdress, and the man wore a mandarin hat. Their heads kept on nodding, and their wise oriental eyes stared straight at Tam. She was so scared that she could not move her feet. She let out one blood-curling yell after the other. The door was flung open. Captain Cromwell rushed in.

"Tam?" he cried. "What happened?"

All Tam could do was point at the accusing Chinese figures, nodding, nodding, and nodding.

"They say I am bad. They say I don't behave properly." She broke down and sobbed.

Captain Cromwell led Tam to a sofa and sat her down beside him. "Why, you poor child, those Chinese figures are not alive. They are made of porcelain. Their heads nod when there is a slight breeze. Come, let me show you."

He stood Tam on a chair so she could see that the heads were fixed on long heavy iron rods that hung inside the hollow bodies. He continued, "They were a gift from a Chinese merchant, and they are very rare and valuable."

By this time they were surrounded by the other children, all eager to have the Chinese figures explained to them. Tam found herself a heroine, because the girls shivered and said they felt just as scared as Tam. To Tam's satisfaction the boys eyed her with admiration. In spite of their velvet suits and lace ruffles, silver buckles and polished dancing slippers, they were still boys who could fight as well as anyone Tam knew in Browne's Lane. Even Henry admitted she had a powerful wallop.

Jeff still wore the dreamy expression that followed Felicity wherever she was. Then it was time to go home.

Sleighs driven by coachmen came to call for the girls and boys. Tam and Jeff would be the only ones to walk home. But Captain Cromwell had ordered his sleigh to be brought out. "Come, Tam and Jeff, I'm driving you home," he said.

Tam's eyes sparkled to think of driving behind those black horses with their jingling bells. Curtsies were made, and Felicity was properly thanked. They went out into the crisp starry night. A three-quarter moon hung over the harbor. It was very still, and the sleigh's runners made music on the hard-packed snow. Tam snuggled under the bearskin robe between Jeff and the captain.

Jeff said that even the President couldn't have had a finer party than Felicity's.

Tam asked why he said President. She would confess her ignorance to Jeff. He was interested in politics and she wasn't. Jeff told her that General Washington had been inaugurated as the very first President of the United States only last spring.

"Well," Tam said, "he hasn't been President very long, so probably people still call him General Washington."

Captain Cromwell agreed that he always thought of him as General Washington.

Tam yawned. It was very late for her to be up. The sleigh came to a stop in Browne's Lane. The diamond panes of the small house showed a light within. Tam thanked the captain for taking her home. Jeff said good night and that he'd see her in school.

Tam went in and found her father and Abigail sleepy-eyed and glad to have her home again. She went to bed at once, saying she would tell about the party in the morning.

Tam told about Felicity's party, but she did not tell how she had punched a boy so hard that his nose bled. But her father heard about it from Captain Cromwell, who had only laughed. The captain was amused. He said, "Tam is the liveliest girl in Salem."

Thomas Morgan, however, was disturbed. That hot temper of Tam's was likely to get her into serious trouble someday if she didn't learn to curb it, he told her. He had been pleased to see what a good influence Abigail had on his wild daughter so far. But right now he had to put the problem out of his mind because Captain Cromwell was very eager to have his brig finished and launched. It had been an open winter, and the carpenters had worked nearly every day.

March came, and the frogs began to peep at night in the marshes. Tam brought home pussy willows for Abigail. Ever since Felicity's party Tam had been very good. She helped with the housework and came directly home when she was sent on errands, but one day spring fever got into her blood and she did not come home after school.

It was an important day because old Aunt Tabby was coming from Marblehead for a day's visit, and Dr. Bentley was coming also. It was to be a neighborhood tea party at Dr. Bentley's request. He liked to meet all his parishioners, not only when they were in trouble but for friendly visiting. Those who did not belong to his parish were invited also. He wanted to make it easier for some of the poorer people around Browne's Lane to entertain him. He would get the people to tell him about old times. Later he would write down all he had heard in his diary. That diary was to make him famous in days to come.

The Collinses, the Bennets, and the Scarlets all contributed something. Butter, fish, potatoes, or corn meal and perhaps some pork. Because Thomas Morgan was a master builder he was not one of the poorer people, and Abigail planned to serve some fancy dishes as a treat. She asked Tam to bring home a canister of China tea, dates, figs, and raisins and to stop in at Widow Adams' for the dainty hearts and rounds that she baked for special occasions. They had been ordered two days ago. Tam promised to do the errand and to come right home from school.

When school was out, Tam heard that everyone was going lickety-split to Market House Square. An elephant was to be exhibited.

"What does it look like?" Tam asked.

Nobody seemed to be sure. But every child was determined to find out. Tam was caught up in the fever of excitement. Not for anything would she miss seeing an elephant. They flew pell-mell out of the schoolyard. The soft smell of spring sent them galloping like colts into the square. A crowd was already there. Tam and Jeff wiggled and squeezed their way through the packed spectators.

There stood a huge animal over six feet high. They gasped at the monstrous dark gray creature. The keeper was feeding him bread and hay. Some men put pieces of bread in their pockets, and the elephant took the bread with his trunk.

Tam trembled with excitement. She picked up a piece of bread and put it in her cloak pocket, but when the elephant's trunk reached out and fumbled in her pocket and looked at her with his little beady eyes, she screamed. It was such a strange uncanny

189

feeling. Jeff thought she was very brave, because he heard that the long ivory tusks reaching beyond the trunk could gore a man and kill him. This made Tam more eager to show off for Jeff.

When the keeper offered to boost anyone up to the elephant's back, only a few men were half willing. But Tam cried out, "Let me get up on his back!" The keeper was delighted. This would make a good spectacle for the mob.

He commanded the elephant to lie down. The huge knees bent. Tam was shoved onto the ornamental saddle blanket that covered part of the elephant's back. She held her breath. The creature began to stand, and she went up, up, higher and higher, and now she looked down at the amazed faces gawking at her.

"Hurrah! Hurrah!" the children yelled. "Look at Tam Morgan!"

The crowd yelled, "Look at the little redhead!"

Her hood had fallen back when the elephant lurched up on his legs. Tam drew a deep breath. It was a glorious feeling to be up on an elephant's back. But the elephant did not agree, and he shook her off. She slid rapidly to the ground and was dumped right into the muddy, trampled earth. Before she got up the elephant filled his trunk with water from a bucket and sprayed it over himself,

and Tam was also doused. She scrambled up, yelling madly and in high spirits. This was wonderful.

The elephant did more tricks. He drank porter, drawing the cork of the bottle and taking the liquor into his throat with his trunk.

It was a long time before Tam was ready to leave the elephant. Jeff said he was hungry and that it was past suppertime.

"Suppertime?" Tam had no idea it was late. "Oh, I hate to leave the elephant," she grumbled, "but I have errands to do."

Jeff snorted, "Errands? All the stores are closed. You'll catch it when you get home, redhead," he teased.

Tam turned on him in a fury. "Why didn't you tell me it was so late?" she demanded.

Jeff said, "I didn't know about your errands. Anyway, you wouldn't have listened to me. All you thought about was the elephant."

Tam began to look so miserable that he said, "Oh, don't worry. Your mother won't care when you tell her about the elephant. She never saw one."

"Oh," Tam moaned, "she will care, and I will be spanked hard because Dr. Bentley is there for a neighborhood tea party and I was to bring our share of the food. Jeff I can't go home. I'll have to stow away on a ship. Let me have some of your clothes and I'll chop off my hair."

They were walking slowly toward home. The streets were jammed with people coming and going. The elephant was all they talked about. Jeff didn't know what to do about Tam.

"I'll go along with you and say it was all my fault that you forgot," he said.

"You would?" Tam's lips went up a bit at the corners. Jeff's devotion warmed her heart.

"That might save me from a spanking, but it wouldn't save Mother from being ashamed because she had nothing for the party."

As they drew closer to the house Tam's feet dragged more and more. "You go home, Jeff. I'll not have you blamed. It is all my fault. I don't remember to keep my promises. The schoolmaster says I have no sense of responsibility, and he is right."

Jeff parted with her reluctantly. "You are a brave girl. I wouldn't dare to face my parents if it was me."

Tam turned into Browne's Lane. The little house seemed quiet. "It must be very late," she mumbled. She braced herself and opened the door, expecting to face the neighbors and Dr. Bentley. But only Abigail and her father were in the room.

Abigail was weeping. Her father was striding up and down the room, and his face was dark with anger.

Tam threw off her hood and cloak.

"Lass," her father said in a stern voice, "how could you disgrace this house? How could you shame your mother?"

Tam's heart broke. She flung herself on the floor and buried her head in Abigail's lap. "I'm sorry," she wailed. "Forgive me. I'll never forget again, never, never." Her voice rose in a cry of anguish.

Abigail laid her hands on Tam's head. Then she gathered her up into her lap. Tam put her arms around Abigail's neck and wept bitterly on her shoulder.

Thomas Morgan stopped pacing the floor. His eyes softened. Tam's repentant sobs made him reluctant to do his duty. But not long after, Tam was spanked thoroughly and sent to bed supperless. She cried herself to sleep.

The next morning a very meek girl went off to school, and the neighbors peering out their windows shook their heads. That wild Tam Morgan was not improving after all.

School was like a prison, now that March had given way to the warm days of April. The schoolmaster was more strict than ever because it would soon be time for the committee men to examine the scholars, and he wanted his school to do him proud.

When Saturday came around Tam hurried off to the shipyard as soon as Abigail gave her permission. This one Saturday, Tam found the sun warmer. It brought out the tingling odor of newly sawed timber. The air was invigorating with the strong smell of pitch, and it was loud with the pounding of hammers. In Shallop Cove the rope-walkers paced up and down, and she could hear their chanting as they walked. Tam drew a deep breath. She loved everything about shipbuilding. Looming up from the ways, the brig was now a solid bulk. The ribs were covered, the decks were laid, and the bulkheads raised. She saw Moses Carter fitting scrollwork on the rail.

Tam yelled, "Hey! When are you going to put on the figurehead?"

He didn't hear her, so she climbed up the staging and made her way to his side. The carpenters greeted her, but they were too busy to stop and chat.

"When are you going to put on the figurehead?" Tam repeated.

Mr. Carter frowned because he did not like to be interrupted. He said shortly, "They are putting up the platform now. Go away, this is no place for children."

Tam was about to rebel. But her resolution to be good was still quite fresh in her mind, so she climbed down and poked around the shipyard. She saw Jeff coming toward her and she greeted him with loud cries of pleasure. But Jeff was in a hurry. He was helping his father and had just been sent home for a tool his father needed. Jeff climbed up the staging and reappeared beside his father.

Tam sat on a pile of lumber and wondered what to do next. She whistled "Up with the Bonnets of Bonnie Dundee." It felt good to sit in the warm sun and have it beat down on her bare head.

She looked out over the harbor, where three ships rode at their moorings. She whistled so loud that she did not hear a soft light voice cry up, "Tam, you whistle just like a bird." Not until a deep voice said, "That's a fine tune, Tam," did she look around. There was Captain Cromwell in his tall beaver hat, and Felicity in her bonnet and scarlet cloak.

Tam invited, "Come up here, Felicity."

Felicity looked at her father. "I'll help you up, Daughter. You stay here with Tam while I see Thomas Morgan. We expect to step a mast today."

Felicity was boosted by her father and pulled up

by Tam's strong arms. She sat on the clean lumber and dangled her legs over the edge. It was a new and delightful feeling to be up on a lumber pile. The girls chattered, and Tam pointed out Mr. Carter's head appearing now and then at the brig's rail.

"Why, there is Jeff too," Felicity exclaimed.

She waved and called in her gentle voice, but above the thunder of hammers no one could hear her. Tam was a little glad that Jeff did not see Felicity. But she did not count on Felicity's determination to win Jeff's attention.

"Let's go up on the brig and surprise Jeff," Felicity said.

Tam stared at her. Felicity was timid and easily scared. She didn't know what it was like for children to climb the staging with its open spaces showing the ground far below. The staging was made for carpenters' long legs and not for children, whose legs were much shorter. Tam could climb easily because she was strong and very nimble.

Felicity, knowing Tam's scorn for her timidity, declared, "I'm not a fraid cat like you said. I'm going to surprise Jeff."

She scrambled down the lumber pile and went toward the staging. She gave one startled glance at the huge bulk of the brig looming above her. It looked scary now.

"Tam——" She forced herself to act bold the way Tam did and not be afraid of anything. Tam never was afraid, except of course of the porcelain Chinese figures. The memory of that afternoon made Felicity giggle to herself.

"Tam," she said again, "how do I start?"

Tam pointed the way. "You climb up here."

"You go first," Felicity said.

Tam started up. She did not like the idea at all and she felt troubled. She looked down at Felicity stretching her legs and hiking up her long clinging skirts. She was slowly climbing up.

"I'm not a fraid cat." Felicity laughed with confidence.

Then Tam began to tremble. A queer feeling shook her heart. She saw a picture in her mind. She saw Felicity lying white and—— Tam's hands tightened on the staging. She looked down. "Go back—go back! Felicity, don't come up, please."

She saw that Felicity was trying to unhook her frock from a rough end of wood. Felicity lost her balance. For an instant she swayed, trying to reach something to hold onto, then she fell through an open space to the ground below. It all happened in the twinkling of an eye. Tam screamed for help. Men came running. Jeff was there, weeping like a small boy. The carpenters laid Felicity on a plank.

A doctor was sent for, and he examined Felicity and said she would have to be carried home on the plank because her leg was broken.

Tam picked up Felicity's bonnet and gave it to the man who would help carry Felicity home. "Take her bonnet with you."

The men lifted the plank to a long dray hitched to two horses. Felicity opened her eyes. She was conscious now. She saw Tam's face stained with tears. She whispered, "It was my fault, Tam—you warned me."

Tam said in a husky voice, "I'm sorry I ever called you a fraid cat. You are a brave girl and a chip off the old block."

They took Felicity home. A hush had spread over the shipyard until the cry "Grog-ho!" went up. The carpenters talked together over their morning grog. "It's that wild Morgan girl who caused the accident," some said. Then they went back to work. Thomas Morgan's face was set in stern lines. He was determined to get the whole thing straight as soon as he saw Tam at home.

Tam's dejected manner when she reached home gave Abigail a start. What had happened now? She drew out the story of Felicity's accident, and Tam began to cry in the telling. Thomas Morgan came in then. Tam took one look at his face, and she knew that she was going to be spanked harder than ever before. But Abigail shook her head at her husband, and he listened after Abigail had let Tam cry until she was through.

"Why do you say it was your fault, Tam?" she asked.

Tam tried to tell it clearly. How Felicity was determined to climb onto the brig to surprise Jeff. "I used to call her a fraid cat, and she said she wasn't, and I could not stop her from climbing on the staging. I felt terribly queer and trembly. Suddenly I knew it was the wrong thing for her to do. I could really see her lying on the ground just as plain. I called out too late to save her."

Tam pressed against Abigail and buried her face in the clean apron tied around Abigail's waist. She was shivering and feeling miserable.

Abigail patted Tam's curls and looked serious. "I'm sorry it happened, but it was not your fault."

Thomas Morgan spoke up. "No, it wasn't your fault, lass. You are like my grandmother. She saw things that were going to happen before they happened, and they were always sad things."

Tam lifted her face to look at him. "Father, I don't like to see sad things before they happen. Someday I'm going to see something wonderful before it happens. I know it. I feel it in my bones."

Thomas Morgan said, "I hope you do. I remember that my grandmother always believed in fairies. She swept the hearth clean before she went to bed and set a pail of clear water upon the hearth for the fairies."

"Tell me more about your grandmother," Tam said. She began to feel better and she knew her father was not going to spank her. Abigail's loving hands calmed her and made her stop trembling.

Thomas Morgan said, "She was a gawsy woman and had a feysome temper." He went on and on. They didn't understand many of the Scottish words he used, and he teased them by talking with a Scottish burr until they laughed so hard that the small boys came in from their play to see what was going on.

Thomas Morgan had to go back to work. After he left, Jeff came to the door with news.

"Felicity will be all right, but she can't walk for a long time. The doctor says she will have to lie in bed until the break is healed. But her mother says that Felicity is not going to have you for a friend because you are a bad influence on her." Jeff hesitated a moment. Then he went on, "She says the same thing about me too."

Tam felt sad. She was sorry for Jeff, but she was sorrier for herself. She had just begun to be truly fond of Felicity and would like to have her for a friend.

"Poor Felicity," Tam said. "Now she won't be able to christen the brig."

If Tam had been jealous before, all her jealousy melted away. "I suppose some friend or relative of Captain Cromwell's will christen the brig."

Tam wanted to console Jeff. She said, "We'll take Felicity some violets as soon as they are out.

203

We can give them to the cook to smuggle up to her, and Mrs. Cromwell will never know we picked them. But Felicity will, I'm sure."

Jeff's disconsolate face was brighter. "Let's go to the woods and see what is up. I have no chores this afternoon, and Father doesn't need me on the brig."

As the days went along the school children in Salem were growing more and more nervous because the time for the schools to be inspected was very near. The schoolmasters were just as nervous and irritable.

It was a fine morning when a solemn procession of ministers, elders, and selectmen came to Tam's school.

They examined the little children first. They recited the alphabet and then the easy syllables, shouting together, "Ab, eb, ib, ub. Ba, be, bi, bo, bu," until they came to Z.

The older children read the Psalter and Testaments. Their copybooks and ciphering books were examined. Now Tam was glad that the schoolmaster had been so strict, because most of the pupils satisfied the committee. They entered on the school records their testimony as to the good behavior and proficiency of the pupils and the fidelity of the master. All this was done between short speeches by the ministers, elders, and selectmen.

The ordeal was over and the procession made their stately way to the next school.

It was lunch time, and there was more noise than ever. The children were so relieved to have the examination over that they each had to make a noise. Tops were spun and marbles were played until the bell rang. No one was very good or attentive in the afternoon, and for once the schoolmaster did not seem to care. When he dismissed them he gave his usual last words: "Go straight home and be civil to everybody you meet."

Tam did not want to go straight home. She wandered along Main Street, looking in the shopwindows. The apothecary's shop with its huge bulging crimson and purple glass jars was next to the post office. The Sign of the Golden Cup had a display of jewelry. The tailor's shop, the barber's shop, and the saddler's shop were passed by. For a moment Tam lingered at the hairdresser's window to look with curiosity at the rolls of false hair some fashionable ladies wore under their own hair to build it up in a high structure.

"Ugh," Tam muttered, and moved on. Nothing interested her very much. Then she stopped at the Frenchman's window. A child's leghorn hat was

displayed, and it was trimmed with artificial cur-
rants, cherries, and plums. Tam pressed her nose
to the glass. Never had she seen fruit so beautiful. Each currant was perfect in its clear, shining
red depths. Each cherry was more delicious-look-
ing than any cherry ever picked from a tree. The
plums were a soft purple blending with reddish
tones, and each plum was covered with a whisper
of frost so delicate that it hardly changed the colors
underneath.

Tam wanted that hat more than she had ever
wanted anything. For the first time in her life she
wanted a hat. She longed to own this creamy-white
leghorn hat with its wide brim and tall crown
trimmed with the fruit. The ladies going in and out
of the shop were fashionable and rich. They had
chaises waiting for them and colored menservants
who spoke to them in warm dark accents of pride
in their mistresses.

Tam sighed. "Felicity's mother could afford to
buy her this hat." She sighed again. "I wish I were
a girl like Felicity, with pretty dresses and satin
slippers like hers." Tam did not know that this was
the moment in her life when she realized that she
was a girl at heart no matter how vehemently she
had declared she wished she were a boy. From now
on her heart would be filled with the ache of grow-

ing up, with its expectations, with its restlessness and its never-ending wishing.

The mood passed, and Tam went along the street. Her feet led to the Cromwells' mansion. She stood at the gate, wanting to go to the back door and ask the cook how Felicity was getting along. She was too bashful, and after staring up at the windows for a while she turned and hurried home.

The gulls screamed overhead. Tam sniffed the air. It smelled of rain. The gulls flying inland were a sure sign of a storm coming up. She stuck her forefinger in her mouth and held it up. The wind came from the east, she could tell, because her wet finger was cooler on the side toward the east. Even now the wind was blowing dust and scraps of paper down the street and tossing the branches of the trees not yet in leaf. She began to run. She felt frisky and hungry.

The storm lasted three days. The tides were very high and the towering waves lashed the shores. Two fishermen's boats went down and the men were drowned and their bodies were washed ashore. Streamers of black crape fluttered on the fishermen's cottages, and Dr. Bentley was very busy with funerals. Then the storm was over and the weather was so mild and lovely that Dr. Bentley felt less sad. There were a number of new babies in

Salem to be christened, and that made him cheerful.

When Dr. Bentley called at the Cromwells' mansion to inquire about Felicity, he found Tam and Jeff peering through the palings of the fence. When he greeted them, Jeff bobbed politely. Tam turned a rebellious scowl at him.

"You are taking those violets to Felicity, I presume?" he said. At the same time he patted Tam on the back and tried to push her ahead of him through the gate.

To his surprise, she stood firmly rooted to the ground.

She said, "We were just going to give the violets to the cook at the back door."

Jeff added, "We are not ever to see Felicity again because we are a bad influence on her."

Dr. Bentley pursed his lips. "Hummm," he said. "Did Mrs. Cromwell blame you for the accident to Felicity?" He looked toward Tam. She nodded.

Dr. Bentley said, "Peg-leg Jeggles saw and heard the whole affair. He told Captain Cromwell that you had called out a warning to Felicity, who was determined to climb up on the brig to surprise Jefferson. Now you just wait here. I'm going to talk to Mrs. Cromwell, and after I get through telling her that you children are not to blame and that I think you are a good influence on that delicate, pindly child, she will change her mind. I'll tell her, too, that I think you both need Felicity's good influence."

Tam had never heard Dr. Bentley so emphatic except in church when he preached about the fire and brimstone of hell. She was so surprised she could hardly believe her ears.

Dr. Bentley trotted up to the front door as if he were a soldier going in to win a battle. He was thinking to himself that this was his big opportunity. Tam needed a girl friend, one as gentle and nicely brought up as Felicity. He had found out that he couldn't interest Tam in his nature walks or in the Singing Society, but she was showing a devotion to Felicity that he was determined to take advantage of.

Tam and Jeff waited to see what was going to happen. For fifteen minutes they stared at the door. Finally Mrs. Cromwell herself opened it and beckoned them to come. They ran up the brick path. Mrs. Cromwell smiled. "Do come in, children. Felicity will be delighted to see you. She has been asking for you every day."

Tam saw Jeff's face break into a happy grin. She was glad to see Jeff look as if a mountain of sorrow had rolled off his back. They were led to Felicity's bedroom. There sat Dr. Bentley, beaming on everyone.

After the violets had been handed to Felicity and she had smelled with pleasure the woodsy fragrance, Tam spoke up with the latest news.

"The figurehead has been bolted onto the stemhead."

Dr. Bentley was surprised to hear a little girl talk just like a shipbuilder. She went on, "The masts are stepped and the painting has begun. Green paint below the water line."

Felicity said, "Father says the work is going along fast. He is eager to sail on her to China. He says he is going to bring back gifts for you and Jeff."

"My!" Tam bounced on her chair. "What will it be? Something pretty to wear?"

Jeff was astonished. This did not sound like Tam. He looked at her sharply. Tam was changing somehow and she looked almost pretty.

Dr. Bentley put in a word: "No doubt the brig will return from her first voyage and be called a 'happy ship.'"

Everyone in Salem knew that a ship with a good captain and an obedient crew earned that distinction at the end of the first voyage.

Tam turned to Dr. Bentley and asked him a question. "Jeff's father said that the figurehead was a felic——" she stumbled. "A felicit"—she couldn't remember that word—"creature."

Dr. Bentley said, "Felicitous?"

"Yes," Tam replied. "What does that word mean?" She added, "Sir."

"The word means 'happily expressed.' Mr. Carter must feel that the figurehead turned out as beautifully as he hoped it would. It is also like the name Felicity, which means 'happiness.'" Dr. Bentley loved to instruct children, and he would have gone on and on if Mrs. Cromwell had not come in to tell Tam and Jeff that visiting time was over.

"You children go down to the parlor. Tea will be served soon."

Felicity thanked them for the violets and begged them to come again and give her the news about the brig. "You will have to tell me all about the launching."

Tam was about to ask who would christen the brig, when Mrs. Cromwell shooed them out.

The children went down the handsome wide stairway and into the east parlor. There were the Chinese figures with their heads perfectly still and their eyes looking far, far away.

"I wonder what they see?" Tam whispered,

because the room made her feel a little solemn.

Jeff was not interested. He was examining some carved ivory figures. "My father would like these," he said.

Then they were called to the dining room for tea. Jeff went along promptly, but Tam lingered. Something held her back. She heard doors opening and shutting. Still she stood fascinated with the Chinese figures. A picture flashed into her mind. She saw it just as plain as day. Her lips curved into a smile and her eyes sparkled. "Is it true? Will it happen?" She murmured the words. The Chinese figures began to nod their heads. "Yes, it is true— it will happen."

"Oh," Tam whispered to them, "now I know. Now I remember."

At that moment Captain Cromwell called from the door, "Tamesine, come in to tea."

Tam turned to him. She knew a secret. She knew something wonderful. Even before the captain knew it.

"Child," he said, "your cheeks are flushed. Have you a fever? Your eyes are so bright." He put his hand on her forehead.

Tam laughed, "I'm fine. I feel awfully good."

Dr. Bentley was at the table, carrying on an out-spoken discourse against two Salem captains who were dealing in slaves and using their ships to transport the slaves.

Tam and Jeff devoted themselves to the milk biscuits, quince and strawberry preserves. They watched Dr. Bentley pour his tea in the saucer to cool it before drinking. His cup was placed on the tiny cup plate beside. Tam had always drunk from a pewter mug, and to see tea drunk from a saucer was new to her. Perhaps it was fashionable, for Captain and Mrs. Cromwell did the same. Tam drank directly from the Nanking china cup, but Jeff drank from the saucer.

The pound cake, sponge cake, and fruit cake in silver baskets were passed around. Then it was time to go home. Dr. Bentley walked with them, and they tried to slow down to keep even with his dignified pace until they turned into another street.

Then Tam cried, "I'll race you to my corner!" They were off like the wind.

School days were over. It was May, and Salem's lilacs were in full bloom. The soft air was drenched with their perfume. Everything was serene in the house in Browne's Lane. Tam cleaned her room under the eaves. She swept the boys' room and picked up the odds and ends that Nathaniel collected. It was nothing but trash, and she dumped it out into the ash bin. But Nathaniel saw her do it and he howled with anger because each bit of leather, iron, or rope was a treasure he had found.

"You are a horrid old redhead. I don't like you." He punched and kicked her. Jamie echoed, "Old redhead. I don't like you either."

Nathaniel reached up and tore off Tam's hair

ribbon. He ran to the hearth and threw it in the blaze.

Tam's temper flared up. She was ready to slap Nathaniel as hard as she could, but she didn't. She remembered her father's words. He had said that her hot temper must be curbed or it would get her into serious trouble someday.

With an effort Tam held back her desire to get even with Nathaniel. She muttered, "I'll get your treasures and put them back. But you need a box to keep them in. I'll ask Peg-leg Jeggles for one. He has empty boxes in the warehouse."

Nathaniel hugged Tam. His eyes were shining with pleasure.

"Oh, Tam, I like you," he cried. Jamie squeezed her. "I like you too," he said.

Tam laughed to see how easy it was to please the boys. If she had given way to her temper and boxed their ears, the house would now be echoing with screams of anger.

Abigail had seen the whole performance from her bedroom. She smiled to herself. Tam, her daughter, and her two sons were all growing up to be kind and loving and considerate of each other. What more could she ask for? She felt that her life was perfect.

But something else was in store for the family.

That evening when Thomas Morgan came home from the shipyard he wore an expression of dazed astonishment. He smiled and smiled. He burst out, "Oh, it's a great honor has come to this family. I hardly know how to tell it."

Abigail ran to him. He put his arm around her. "Come to me, lass." He held out his hand, and Tam sprang to stand within the circle of his other arm. The boys clung to his legs. Abigail said, "What is it? What is it, Thomas?"

Tam said nothing. She looked across the room with far-seeing eyes. She knew what her father was about to say. Thomas Morgan's voice was that of a man who did not quite believe his good fortune. At last he got it out. "Captain Cromwell requests that Tamesine Morgan christen the brig. His daughter is not able to be present, and she wants Tam to take her place. Next week."

"Oh!" Abigail sang out with joy. "Our Tam, our Tam!"

Her father shook Tam. "What have you to say, lass? Why so silent, lambie?"

Tam lifted her face. "Father, I told you that I would know something wonderful before it happened, and I knew I would christen the brig the day I went to visit Felicity."

Thomas Morgan was thoughtful. "I have heard

it said long ago in Scotland that a child no longer has this gift, if gift it be, when she grows into a young girl. It is better so."

Tam was dreamy. She didn't care to see into the future. She only wanted to look pretty and fashionable like Felicity now that she was to take her place and christen the brig.

"I haven't anything good enough to wear," she declared.

Her father roared. "Just like a woman. Ha, my lass is growing up."

Abigail said, "We'll go shopping, Tam. I'll have to have help to sew a new frock. Maybe Mrs. Carter and Prudence will help. They are excellent seamstresses, and you'll need slippers and stockings and——"

Tam broke in: "I saw a hat in the Frenchman's window that I want if it isn't too costly."

Her father declared, "You may buy anything you want. Captain Cromwell deserves the prettiest outfit possible for this great occasion. But, lass"—he was puzzled—"what is the brig to be named? I have not yet heard."

Tam teased, "It is a secret. You woke me from a dream just before I was to christen a ship, and I couldn't remember the name. But now I remember. I will tell it to Captain Cromwell, and he will promise to keep it a secret from even Felicity."

It was May 26, and the tide would be full at noon. Salem was jammed with people who had come all the way from Cape Ann to Lynn to see Captain Cromwell's brig launched. The shipyard was swarming with people. In the harbor a number of ships anchored within viewing distance were loaded with spectators on the watch. Lumber piles were crowded with people, and boys perched on roofs or any place where they could get a foothold. A special stand had been built for the ministers and other important people and the relatives of Captain Cromwell.

Jeff and his friends prowled under the grandstand. From the ground the brig looked immense. The copper sheathing rose in a curve above them, and they had to lean 'way back in order to see the rails of the ship. They couldn't see the flags and bunting that trimmed the stays.

The carpenters were busy at the most exciting part of their work. They greased the timbers with mutton tallow to make it easy for the ship to slide into the water when the blocks were knocked away.

Jeff saw his father dressed in his fine old wedding clothes. He was among the honored guests. The figurehead leaned forward, waiting for the moment when her body would feel the first dash of cold water.

"I wonder where Tam is?" Jeff said to himself. He left the boys, who had decided to climb on a roof. A band began to play. Thomas Morgan gave a signal for his men to commence knocking the blocks away. Jeff ran as fast as he could. Tam must be getting ready for her great moment.

In the meantime, Tam was leaving the house along with Abigail. She wore a white frock of embroidered muslin with a short waist and short puffed sleeves. Her slippers were soft black kid, and the leghorn hat with its trimming of gorgeous artificial fruit was tied under her firm round chin.

Nathaniel strutted in his first breeches. Jamie had inherited Nathaniel's best skirts, and he was very proud.

Captain Cromwell drove up in his chaise and helped them into it. They drove off in style to the platform where Tam would stand.

Then Captain Cromwell gave Tam a bottle of Madeira wine all tied about with silver paper and fluttering ribbons. Tam exchanged a mischievous smile with him. Soon everybody would know their secret.

The noise of the mauls stopped, and there was silence. Tam, with her amber-colored eyes sparkling, swung the bottle of wine against the brig. There was a sharp sound of cracking glass, and Tam was saying in her loudest voice, "I christen thee The *Felicity!*"

A cheer went up. The name was repeated from mouth to mouth, "The *Felicity!*"

Dr. Bentley pronounced the benediction. Then with the last few swings of the mauls against the blocks, the brig felt the thrill of life along her keel and began gently slipping down the ways. She gained speed and everybody yelled, "Hurrah! Hurrah!"

A cannon from the hill saluted the *Felicity*. The church bells pealed like mad, and the band played "Hail, Columbia."

The brig struck water. The figurehead took her baptism of salt water with serene grace. More cannon were shot off, and then the *Felicity* was floating free in the harbor and all the little boats bobbed in her wake, as was proper and respectful.

Tam held the neck of the wine bottle with its festoon of ribbons. "I'm going to keep this forever and ever," she declared.

Captain Cromwell led the Morgans to the grandstand so everybody could meet Tam. Abigail was proud of the way Tam made her manners. Captain Cromwell had invited his close friends for dinner to celebrate the launching. He could not persuade Thomas Morgan to give up one hour of his time, for now he was anxious to get the rigging done and the finishing touches added. After that the *Felicity* would be furnished with all the provisions needed for her first voyage.

Tam saw Jeff wiggling through the crowd to join his father. She would meet him later at the Cromwell mansion. She wondered if he would think she was as pretty as Felicity. She wondered if he would like her more this way, all dressed up, than he did when she was his harum-scarum companion. Then she wondered what Felicity would say when she heard the brig had been christened for her. Tam had a warm, cozy feeling around her heart as she thought of the greatest pleasure of all, telling the big news to Felicity.

Then she giggled because Captain Cromwell said, "You look so proper and just like a young lady, Tam. What has become of the liveliest girl in Salem?"

Tam tipped back her head, and from under the wide brim of the leghorn hat he saw an impudent grin.

"She is right here!" Tam cried.

Tam scampered up the broad stairs to Felicity's room. She found her sitting up in bed.

"Tam!" Felicity cried out. "How pretty you look. Tell me quick all about the christening."

Tam pushed back her hat, and it hung down her back. She grinned. "I have a secret to tell you."

Tam bent down and whispered the name she had christened the brig. Then she stood up and watched Felicity's radiant smile. Felicity held out her arms, and the girls hugged each other. They chattered and laughed and giggled until Captain Cromwell came to stand at the foot of the stairs. He smiled to himself. He had a feeling that the girls were going to be wonderful friends.